I0720429

FALLING THROUGH THE NEW WORLD

A NOVEL IN STORIES

BY THE SAME AUTHOR

Badlands

The Last Whaler

FALLING THROUGH THE NEW WORLD

A NOVEL IN STORIES

BY CYNTHIA REEVES

gold wake

"...turn Your gaze to our brothers and sisters who,
far from their beloved homeland and from all that
is dearest to them, are forced to struggle in the
midst of serious difficulties..."

FALLING THROUGH THE NEW WORLD

PART I: THE OLD WORLD

LA DOLENTISSIMA MADRE

At the deserted kitchen table Mamma ties a wide ribbon of my handmade lace around a gold box. She winds each of the two long strands trailing from the knot around her fingers, once, twice, three times, and secures the center with a piece of thin wire. The bow's petals fall like those of a chrysanthemum as she fluffs them into a pleasing circle of overlapping loops. To make each loop requires ten centimeters of ribbon; to make each centimeter of ribbon requires a quarter turn of the clock. In the time it takes Mamma to fashion the bow, she has used up another day of my life.

Mamma wraps a fistful of almond *confetti* in tulle and attaches it to the ribbon with a straight pin. I finger a petal of the lace. The pattern is called *torchon*: a rose ground with an edge of repeating fans. It is the one Sister Benedict was teaching me to make before my brother, Antonio, returned home from the Great War. There are imperfections in the lace—a weaver's knot unraveling and a rose missing one of its stitches. I worry the knot as if the mistakes can be undone. Mamma taps my hand.

"The bow was perfect," she scolds. "Now look at it."

Does she believe the bow will stay exactly as she tied it throughout her pilgrimage to the mountaintop friary? Does she believe the gift will earn plenary indulgences from Brother Romano? Does she believe her prayers can turn the clock backwards?

Mamma removes her apron and stands in the middle of the kitchen clad only in a slip. She does not care that Antonio is in the corner, watching her. She thinks he cannot see her. She pulls on her best dress, navy wool with pearl buttons running down the back.

"Come, Anna, help me fasten these."

I slip each rounded button through its narrow buttonhole, then secure the gold clasp of the three-strand pearl necklace Papà gave her when they married. She twists her long, damp hair into a chignon, secures it with two rhinestone pins, and imagines, perhaps, Brother Romano's delighted smile, the sympathy in his eyes, even the touch of his hand on her cheek. She thinks that I do not understand even these small things.

"You aren't attending a dignitary's funeral," I say quietly as she licks her index finger and pastes a stray wisp of hair to her widow's peak.

She clucks her tongue. "*You* should learn to show the same respect. These are holy men, closer to God than we are."

"Is it because they live on the mountain?" I ask, my voice sprinkled with sugar.

In response, she adjusts each pleat of her dress into a perfect crease, though I ironed each one sharp as a knife this morning. "I must be well for Papà and Antonio."

Stay, I want to tell her.

"Prayers are all the medicine my dear Ernestina needs," she says. I can see Mamma standing in front of me—was it just this morning?—adjusting each pleat of her dress into a perfect crease. "You're young and strong. If you get sick, you'll recover."

"That's what you told Ernestina."

She slaps me hard across the face. "What's happened to you?"

My cheek burns. Mamma drapes a cream-colored veil on her head without saying another word. I turn away before she can see my involuntary tears. When I turn back, she has already disappeared through the front gate, leaving behind a dust blossom rising from the path, the bloom of three red fingers on my cheek.

"Stay," I say out loud. But what is the point of talking to dust?

*   *   *

The wood has gone gray in the kitchen hearth. I tap the spent logs with an iron poker until the embers glow red, shovel the cinders into the ashcan, then add fresh kindling and cypress logs. New tongues of fire leap up as the wood touches hot coals. The fire catches and burns and dies down to low flames. I hang our large cast-iron pot on the hook and push it over the heat.

While I tend the fire, Antonio works at the table, scoring a rind of pork fat. He cuts a perfect grid in the surface and pounds garlic and fresh herbs into the rind, white and glistening, smooth as cream. He is sweating from the effort of beating the lard to a soft pulp for the gravy. *Woman's work*, Mamma would say if she could see him. But she will not see him. I take the knife from his hands and push him toward Papà's chair. He needs his rest.

The lard spits and crackles when I throw it into the heated iron pot. It melts quickly, coating the bottom with a thick layer of grease. I stir in onion and garlic and add the pork Papà has brought in from the smokehouse.

Papà kisses me on the forehead and watches me choose the ripest tomatoes from the windowsill.

"What do you think?" I ask him, holding up one tomato with a deep brown gash.

"You, too, must find time to rest," he says, nodding toward Antonio, who is rocking rhythmically by the quiet fire. He takes the scarred tomato from my hand and bites through its flesh. "It's perfect," he says, and stuffs it into his mouth.

Papà knows there is no time for rest. Meals must be made, the laundry washed, hung, and taken down from the line. He will not rest until after the olive harvest. I will not rest until my sister, Ernestina, recovers from the influenza, or dies. Even when I sit, my mind burrows into one black flower and the next. A garden of black flowers, each needing its special tending.

I chop the tomatoes and add them to the pot, then wipe the

perspiration from my brow with the corner of my apron. *Yes, rest, Antonio*, I think as he rocks. *Rest for both of us.* But he does not rest. He sits in Papà's favorite chair and counts. Fingers, toes, coins. When there is nothing left to count, he will etch a mark in the yellowed kitchen plaster, tally all the days since his return from the military hospital where he had been treated for burns and the effects of phosgene gas. Ninety-one scars line the wall.

*   *   *

Papà paces the aisles in our olive grove, pinching select fruit to check for ripeness. He hopes to rescue each olive at the peak of its flavor, but before the flies damage too much of his precious crop. The females like to bore holes in the soft skin of the olives, secrete their eggs inside the ripening ovals, and in doing so, destroy them without meaning to.

The flies have been especially difficult this year because of the prolonged heat, summer stretching into fall as it sometimes does, even though Papà's family, according to custom, soaked the seeds and cuttings in the juice of house-leek before planting them. Papà no longer believes in these old superstitions. He has spent two weeks tending to the lighted smoke pots, adding dung and sulfur and ox horn to drive away the pests. The smoke drifts windward, away from the house and up into the mountains. I spy him through the kitchen window, weaving between columns of smoke and the wide rows of trees along the paths he has worn with worry, pausing here and there in his lonely pilgrimage to kneel in the dirt to tend the pots. He does not stop to watch innumerable ashes rise like black stars into the black sky. His lone concern is the harvest.

This fall, it seems, one pestilence follows another. First the drought, and now the flies. Papà calls it his agony in the garden, but this is not his only sorrow. Each night when he comes in, his eyes are red. He tells me it is merely the irritation of smoke and ash.

At the well by the edge of the grove, Papà helps me draw

two buckets of fresh water. "I wish I could do something more, *carissima*," he says, stroking my cheek. "It wasn't always like this. It won't always be like this."

I say nothing because I do not wish to discourage him or to acknowledge his lie. He vanishes, head down, into the maze of trees and smoke. Saving the grove keeps him busy night and day in the fall. He worries that he will fail these trees, which have passed through several generations of his family. He does not wish to disappoint his dead father. But more than this, he is afraid of Mamma, her shrill tongue, her wounding silences.

*   *   *

I imagine Mamma on her pilgrimage, walking beneath the cathedral of ilex and holm oak along the old mule-path that leads up to the friary. She brings gifts to the friars almost every day now. Our fresh-pressed olive oil in corked bottles. Miniature *cornetti* crowned with homemade vanilla cream. Sheep's milk pie dotted with shaved chocolate and candied orange peel. Today's *baci* are Brother Romano's favorite. I stirred melted bittersweet chocolate into hazelnut butter, and she dipped the soft balls one by one into more bittersweet, the *baci* soft kisses we wrapped in bits of wax for the friars, kisses for the friars we wrap in wax so that they will have sweet where our lives are bitter.

"Fair exchange for Brother Romano's prayers," she said, ticking off on her fingers the miracles she attributes to his intercession. "They brought Antonio back from the war. They cured his influenza. They may likewise spare Ernestina and bring back your beloved Vincenzo."

Her words remind me that my husband has yet to return from the Austrian prison camp where he's been held for the past year. I have had no word since the war ended. Antonio's return, damaged as he still is, gives me hope.

Mamma shampooed her hair in the kitchen tub while Papà, Antonio, and I ate our morning *pagnottine* and washed them down

5

with thick, black espresso. I brought a hot roll and cold water to Ernestina. Even the aroma of fresh-baked bread was not enough to arouse her hunger, but she was grateful for the water, the cool washcloth on her forehead, my hand laid on her shoulder.

There is always some new ache requiring a fresh string of prayers. Mamma is ever ready with her rosary. The friars think Mamma is a saint. Brother Romano lights a candle every morning for her. Each candle burns until nothing is left but the silver disk that holds the charred wick. I have been to the friary chapel with Mamma many times. I have watched the candles burn themselves out.

*   *   *

By now, Mamma must have reached the first of five shrines that mark the path up the mountain. Each shrine has a statue of the Virgin, each Virgin housed in an alcove brimming with browning flowers and holy cards of the dead and tiny scrolls of the living. Spare us this and spare me that, the parchments say. Litany of sufferings, indulgences of the damned. To pass the time, I often read these silent petitions while she prays. She says I am incorrigible. She says such intentions are private. But they are all the same. I imagine the Virgin picking among the scraps of paper, pulling up her chair before her husband, begging Him for mercy. How does she choose whom to favor with His blessings? To whom does the cup pass?

Mamma kneels at the first shrine. This is the statue whose arms are open in welcome, whose face gazes down on the supplicant with benevolent calm. The statue has spoken to me on more than one occasion.

"*Dilettissima Annina*," the Virgin says, "how is your suffering greater than mine?"

"How can one compare sufferings?" I ask her. "It's like comparing the five wounds of Jesus. Are they measured by depth or breadth?"

For these questions, I receive no answer. I am presumptuous, Mamma tells me. My words are a sacrilege. I will burn in hell for all eternity. And so on and so forth. It is the same thing every day.

I imagine Mamma blessing herself with the wooden cross of her rosary and praying the Apostles' Creed, followed by three Hail Marys whose beads tick off the divine virtues of faith, hope, and love, and then the Glory Be. She announces her intention to the Virgin: to contemplate the Sorrowful Mysteries. No matter that it is Saturday, a day for the Joyful Mysteries—annunciations and angel's visits, nativities and turtle doves, losing a son and finding him again.

—What harm can it do, Anna, to reflect on Jesus' suffering seven days a week?

—Perhaps if we meditated on joy, Mamma, we'd have joy.

But of course she cannot hear me. She does not hear me even when she is in front of me.

—I watched my Son suffer, the Virgin tells her.

—I, too, watched my son suffer, and through your gracious intercession, he was spared a fate less harsh than your Son's. She pauses. —There is one more thing.

—I gave you my Son. What more could you ask of me?

—Perhaps if you'd had a daughter, you'd understand how this suffering is worse.

The Virgin is silent. Does Mamma realize that she has gone too far? She bends her forehead to the ground and speaks to the dust. —The first Sorrowful Mystery is the mystery of doubt, Christ's agony in the garden. She holds the first single bead and recites, —Our Father, who art in heaven...

Is it doubt that causes her suffering?

—Hail Mary, full of grace...

Mary looks down on Mamma from her cement niche. In the Virgin's submissive bearing, Mamma sees an example for herself.

—Lord, she prays, let it be done to me according to Thy word.

She counts each new bead of the rosary until she reaches

the end of the first decade. Fingering the single ending bead, she recites, —Jesus, have mercy on us. Forgive us our sins. Save us from the fires of hell. Take all souls into heaven, especially those most in need of Thy mercy.

She dips her fingers in the holy water font, which has been empty for months. Rainwater keeps the font filled, and there has been little rain. She blesses herself with a dry sign of the cross and leaves at the Virgin's feet a gaudy purple mum from a spray of wild mums she has picked along the path.

*   *   *

Antonio emerges from the cellar cradling five eggs in his shirt. He hands them to me, one by one, and I wipe the ashes from the shells. Just yesterday, it seems, Ernestina and I prepared the eggs for winter storage by polishing the shells with lard and dusting them with ashes from Papà's smudge pots. That day, she smeared a fatty ashen cross on my forehead and said, in her best Father Gaetano impression, "Remember, Annina, that thou art dust." The lard made the ashes especially indelible—I wore a black cross on my forehead for two days afterward.

The hens last laid eggs in early October. Could a month have passed since that afternoon in the kitchen?

Five eggs, five large handfuls of flour, five pinches of salt. A measure for each of us. Ernestina will not be able to eat her portion, but five eggs is a habit I will find hard to break. I make a well in the middle of the flour.

"Go ahead, Antonio," I say, taking his battle-scarred military helmet from his head and placing it gently on the table. He kneels at the table and examines the first egg. He says there is a weakness in every shell, a spot thinner than the rest, more susceptible to cleanly breaking. He taps this egg with the edge of his fingernail and runs the nail around the egg so that the shell is hardly damaged. He picks up each egg in turn and repeats the process. While I beat the eggs and slowly stir them into the flour, he reassembles each shell. Five empty shells, smeared with ash, sit side by side on the table. Soon I have a ball of dough to knead.

"*Uno, due, tre,*" he mumbles.

"*Quattro, cinque, sei,*" I respond.

I punch and fold the dough into itself, letting him pace my work. What harm can it do? The recipe calls for one hundred kneads, though I can tell when I am finished by the feel of the dough. *Settanta, ottanta, novanta, cento.*

"Sit," I say, nudging him into Papà's chair.

"*Cento, cento, cento,*" he sings with his hands raised in the air.

*　　*　　*

By now, Mamma has reached the second shrine, the one where Mary cradles the baby Jesus. The boy is reaching up to the sky as if trying to catch something paler than air. This was Antonio, before the war, lifting up Mamma when he was happy. It is hard to imagine this baby Jesus as a man stripped and beaten.

—The second Sorrowful Mystery is the scourging at the pillar, she announces. Her voice falters. She clears her throat. —Our Father, who art in heaven...

She meditates on the torment the Son endured. "Thirty-nine stripes, the mortification of His flesh," Father Gaetano intones during every Good Friday service. "The flesh is dead, and still this furious whipping was not enough suffering to redeem the world."

Sister Benedict says that men are too much focused on the torture, not enough on the salvation. She imitates the grave words of our village priest—*we must mortify ourselves before the Lord in order to be healed*—as I repeat row after row of perfect stitches under her tutelage. Mamma cannot see Sister Benedict slapping her hand on one shoulder and then the other, mocking Father Gaetano's words. Mamma does not see the thirty-nine marks on Jesus' back. Mamma sees only a baby reaching for the sky. She asks Him to aid those most in need of His mercy. She means herself.

*　　*　　*

The kitchen grows warmer as the day wears on. The heat from the coals, the rays of the sun through the window, the binding of my apron strings. Everything feels too close. Beads of perspiration fall from my chin onto the ball of pale yellow dough as I oil it and set it aside to rest. I blot the sweat with my apron, groping blindly for the seat of a kitchen chair. I sit to wait for this vertigo to pass. Then Ernestina's faint voice comes from our shared bedroom.

"*Annina*," she whispers as I enter her room, "*ho sete*."

I am thirsty.

Her cheeks are streaked with the red of violent heat and thin smears of blood. I do not understand this influenza, how suddenly it comes on. Two days ago she helped me take down crisp white sheets, scented with autumn air, from the outside line. Today she is wrapped in those same sweet sheets, soaked in sweat and blood.

Waves of heat rise from her body as I smooth fresh sheets around her and place a cool, wet washcloth on her forehead. Her eyes—two shades of brown, like melted chocolate stirred in earth—flutter open, then close. She moans softly as I press my fingers to her forehead. When I was a child, she soothed my thousand lesser sufferings by holding me in her lap and stroking my hair. I can still hear the crystal bell of her voice. *Dolcissima sorella*—sweetest sister, dissolving on her tongue as if my name were a confection lighter than air. Now when she speaks, her voice comes low and far away, like the timbre of funeral bells pealing daily at San Ponziano.

"Mamma," she whispers even more softly, "*ho sete*." Are these twin longings all that is left of my sister?

—The third Sorrowful Mystery is the crowning with thorns, the mystery of faith. Our Father, who art in heaven, hallowed be Thy name...

—But Mamma, she's thirsty.

—Say the prayer with me, Anna.

—...forgive us our trespasses as we forgive those who trespass against us. And lead us not into temptation, but deliver us from evil. Amen.

She places a wild yellow mum at Mary's feet and blesses herself from the font of no water.

—The pitcher is empty.

—Then go to the well.

—And there is still the laundry...

The world goes black for a second. I press my forehead on the bedroom's cool plaster wall and close my eyes. Is it possible to fall asleep standing up as I have heard?

—The pleats are perfect, Mamma, perfect. I ironed them myself, sharp as knives.

But it is not Mamma in my shadows. It is Ernestina with a flush on her cheeks that I mistake for health, chiding me for daydreaming over the padded laundry table full of linens. She places her hand over mine, lifts the iron that I have left too long on Mamma's favorite tablecloth, and examines the triangular scorch mark with her elegant fingers.

"Dear Annina," she says as we fold the cloth just so, to hide the burn from Mamma. "Who is it this time? Mario? Ettore?"

"You know it's always Vincenzo," I reply.

"He's in our prayers. Your beloved will come back from the war, just as Antonio did."

"Your Michele didn't," I say, too sharply. Can I snatch those words back from the blackness?

I drop my end of the tablecloth and run inside the house. And inside the house, inside this dream of a dream, there is Vincenzo, cowering in the trenches, holding his arms against the falling sky. There is Vincenzo, lifting his battered boots, one foot in front of another, through deep mountain snow. There is Vincenzo, marking, marking, marking the prison barrack's wall.

No, I did not apologize for my temper. Such an insignificant thing between sisters.

I go to the well for fresh water. The rope squeals on the

pulley as I raise the full bucket hand over hand. Cupping the cool water, I splash my face. The November sun is weak, but I am perspiring.

*   *   *

Antonio sits at the kitchen table, waiting for Papà to come in with the day's olives, carving intricate lines into the table-top with his fingernails. His hands move constantly over the surface. A shallow pattern of alternating diamonds and curves unfurls like a tablecloth made of wooden lace.

"Beautiful," I say, urging him to continue. The gravy simmers over the banked red coals. The whole house smells of garlic and onions and the lingering odor of sauteed lard and pork. I spoon a generous portion of meat and gravy into a bowl and offer it to him.

"What do you think, does it need more salt?" I ask.

He blows across the spoon and takes a sip. "*Superbo!*" he says, then takes a bite of pork.

His cheeks betray the ruddy glow of physical health, but in the depths of his illness, my brother would cover his emaciated face with crossed arms and scream, "The sky is falling," cock-of-the-walk in the Italian fairy tale, reduced to tears. I tell myself it is a matter of care, of waiting. Ernestina tended Antonio when he came back to us, a ghost unknowingly infected with the influenza. She changed his sheets and covered his forehead with cool cloths and shooed me out of his bedroom.

"Go, Annina," she told me. "Go help Papà."

We did not know then the nature of this sickness. We did not know how something we could not see could do such harm. How each neighbor would turn away from us when they heard Antonio was taken ill. That our family would be left alone, and each of us in turn alone, like those painted nesting dolls so precisely shaped that each one in succession hides exactly within the next.

Antonio licks the bowl clean.

"What would Mamma say if she saw that?"

"Don't tell Mamma, and I shall tell you that the gravy is—" and he kisses his bunched fingers with a loud smacking sound.

"Oh, Antonio," I say, touching his arm. "Ernestina's is better."

He looks down at the place on his arm where my hand rests, then jerks away from me as if I have slapped him there. His skin still peels where the fires burned him. As he waits for Papà, he pulls pieces of dead skin from his arms and arranges them in neat piles on the table. They are hills of ash.

*   *   *

What is the difference between hosanna and crucify? I imagine Jesus riding triumphantly into Jerusalem along the palm-strewn path, All Hail King of the Jews, and, not one week later, Jesus carrying His olive-wood cross along the very same road to the place of the skull. A pitcher of water, a box of kisses, dung for the smudge pots, all carried along the same road. We stop along the way to comfort our friends, to pray for our enemies. We leave our faces as shadows in a compassionate woman's veil. We tell our families not to weep for us but only for themselves and their children. We dry our eyes, all but Mamma. She cries now, she cries at Mary's feet. This is the Mary with her hands parted, her eyes raised up to heaven. It is the Mary who is looking directly at God. Mamma saves her dearest prayers for this Mary. She lights a votive candle, which wavers behind red glass like flowing blood.

—The fourth Sorrowful Mystery, she whispers, is the mystery of suffering. Jesus carries the cross through the streets of Jerusalem on His way to Calvary.

She believes the tears she sheds are gifts for God, water for the font.

—I don't ask anything for myself, she prays, only for others. What happened this morning? Make Anna more obedient. You know I've done everything in my power to bend her to Your will. I've been reduced to hitting her! What else? Oh yes. Send us rain for the olive grove. Let Antonio stop his dreadful counting. If it's Your will, please spare my dearest Ernestina.

Mamma is the model of obedience, prostrate before this shrine, reciting her ten Hail Marys to the dust.

—And if, she says finally, but this time so softly it is a whisper within a whisper only God can hear, and if it's instead Your will, please take my sweet daughter straight to heaven. It would be a comfort to know that she's spared the uncertainty of purgatory.

She makes her wildflower offering, her parched cross of water.

*　　*　　*

Papà and Antonio pick out twigs and stray silver-green leaves as they sort olives from a large basket into several smaller baskets according to color. The choicest ones will be taken to the press; the others I will preserve in oil and spices for the coming winter.

Antonio counts the olives in each basket and tallies the count on a slate board he scratches with chalk, marks so faint only he can see them. I touch his hands so that his mind might rest.

"There's no harm in his counting," Papà chides me. He gathers the discarded olive branches into vases and places them around the room. He thinks this will somehow reduce our suffering. "When he's finished his counting, we'll all be dead but Mamma."

Even Antonio laughs at my father's favorite joke.

"Who can blame Mamma for being scared?" Papà says to me as I wipe the tears from my eyes.

He must say such things. He is tied to Mamma for life, but I am not. I will no longer count the beads of her rosary like so many hours in a day.

*　　*　　*

Papà brings the basket of choicest olives to the factory behind our house. The millstone turns and crushes the olives to pulp, which falls in a thick stream to the copper tub underneath. He carries the tub to the oil press, layers paste and sheets of woven *fiscoli* like a thin-tiered wedding cake, and stacks them on an iron pole. I have watched our mule circle the pressing machine. The filters squeeze and squeeze together, yielding liquid emerald from the paste.

*　*　*

I pick up Mamma's kitchen knife and fit my hand in the grooves worn by our fingers. I score the buttery smooth dough with evenly spaced slits, which part like skin, only there is no blood. Using the slits as a guide, I slice the dough into rounds and roll out each round into a thin sheet.

Antonio rises from Papà's chair and sits at the kitchen table. He touches my cheek where Mamma's fingerprints are fading. He has seen everything. He has seen worse things.

I give him the child's jobs—to dust the *strangozzi* with flour as I cut the thin sheets of dough into strips, and to hang the pasta on wooden racks to dry.

"Truly you don't need to count them," I say to him, catching the longing in his eyes. "There's more than enough."

I take his hands away from the hanging strands and place them near the pile of flour. We watch the strands regain the perfect symmetry of parallel lines. I work more quickly, the knife edge a silver blur. The knife falls and falls and falls. I do not notice the gravy boiling over onto the red-hot embers. Flames shoot up as the melted lard from the gravy rekindles the fire.

Antonio grabs his helmet and ducks under the kitchen table. He mumbles to himself, a prayer, an oath, something I cannot make out as I throw cold ash onto the flames. More of the gravy boils over, sending a plume of flame nearly up to my hand. I hurry to remove the pot from the fire with the pothook, while more flames leap up from the coals.

"Dreczenca is burning! Dreczenca is burning!" he cries from underneath the table. In the reflection of the innocent kitchen flames, he sees the flames that lit up the sides of the mountain near Caporetto.

"You're home, Antonio!" I shout at him, dumping the whole can of ashes over the flames. The fire sputters and dies. My hands, my apron, everything is covered with ash.

"Come out," I say, reaching my hand under the table. "You see, the flames are gone."

His head is down. He is shaking. I clasp his hands together with mine and pray, "*Kyrie eleison, Christe eleison, kyrie eleison.*"

But what is mercy? He will not come out. His eyes are afire, the whites streaked with narrow red veins, ancient eyes staring at me from his young man's body. He does not believe me. I place my hand over his eyes, gently, to close them. That is mercy.

* * *

Ernestina calls for Mamma again, but I go to her side. She cannot tell the difference between Mamma and me, which is a blessing. She no longer coughs up the blood and phlegm clogging her lungs. The doctor has told us that when she dies, she will suffocate in her own breath.

I bathe her lips with water.

"Oh," Ernestina whispers, "it's sour."

But it is her own blood she tastes. She begins to moan and thrash, tangling herself in the sheets. "You're trying to poison me, Mamma."

"No, no," I soothe, holding her body down until she quiets.

It is time to call Father Gaetano. He will not come, as he did not come for Antonio when he was ill with the same fever. He told us, "The needs of the flock outweigh the needs of one suffering sheep."

To which Ernestina responded, "How think ye? If a man have a hundred sheep, and one of them be gone astray, doth he not leave the ninety and nine, and goeth into the mountains, and seeketh that which is gone astray?"

I have never seen a holy man so angry. Holy man, so close

to God he can almost touch His robes.

I am not a man. I am not a priest. I am not qualified to perform the rite my sister requires in this most extreme urgency. Sister Benedict has told me her God is merciful. It is to this God I turn. With our finest olive oil, I make the sign of the cross on Ernestina's forehead. I repeat the words Ernestina prayed over Antonio. "Through this holy unction and His own most tender mercy, may the Lord pardon thee whatever sins or faults thou hast committed."

I anoint each of Ernestina's hands.

"Is this sacrilege, Mamma?" I ask as I imagine Mamma reaching the last shrine.

—The fifth Sorrowful Mystery, she says, is the Crucifixion of our Lord, the mystery of death, the mystery of eternal life. In the name of the Father, and of the Son, and of the Holy Ghost.

The doleful Virgin—the dead Christ draped over one arm, a closed fist on her breast—looks down from her cave-like grotto. We call this one "*la dolentissima madre*." This is the mother who will anoint Jesus' five wounds and the thirty-nine lashings with the oil of olives and balsam, who will cover His face with a fine cloth and wrap His body in a linen shroud, who will lay Him in a borrowed tomb. This is the mother who cannot stop weeping though her Son has told her not to weep for Him. This is the mother who has almost forgotten the promise of the Resurrection.

I dip my hands in the oil again and bless my sister's eyes, nose, ears, lips. Then I break a sliver from her untouched breakfast roll. "The body and blood of Christ," I say, gently pushing the wafer into her mouth and giving her a sip of water.

Is this sacrilege, Mamma? I think.

Through the window, I see the clouds thicken, darken, blot out the sun. Could a storm be imminent? I must tell Papà to come in from the rain. I must take the laundry down from the line. Mamma will be caught in the downpour, her veil bedraggled, her hair loosened from the rhinestone pins. What will Brother Romano think? What will become of his box of kisses?

Looking up at the threatening sky, Mamma hurries through the final beads of the rosary and reaches the joiner. I can almost see her fumbling with the cross, debating on another chaplet. She watches the sky darken further and breathes in the odor of dying leaves and cypress and dampening earth. She returns her gaze to the Virgin and says the final prayer, —Hail Holy Queen, Mother of mercy, our life, our sweetness, our hope.

I refresh the washcloth and wipe the blood coming from Ernestina's nose. "Mamma is here," I say.

—Pray for us, oh Mother of God, Mamma says.

"That we may be made worthy of the promises of Christ," I respond automatically.

Mamma blesses herself with the cross, kisses the dead Christ's feet, and places the last of her wildflowers there.

The rain begins to fall in earnest. Mamma, safe under the Virgin's alcove, changes into the fresh stockings and shoes she has carried in her bag. She cups her hand out into the falling rain and drinks. Those first drops taste sweet.

*　　*　　*

I soak the bloodied washcloth in cool water and place it over my face. It is too hot for late November. It is too hot to move. I lie down in my bed next to Ernestina's and imagine Mamma carefully sliding the lace ribbon from the box of *baci*. She lifts the lid and chooses one of the plumper chocolates, then rearranges the remaining kisses so that, she thinks, the absence will not be missed. She slips the ribbon onto the box, fluffs the bow, and waits with her *baci* and her prayers for the rain to pass.

*　　*　　*

I must close my eyes, but who will care for my sister? Mamma says she must stay well for Papà and Antonio. Mamma says her prayers are all the medicine Ernestina needs.

She is standing right in front of me, adjusting each pleat

18

of her dress into a perfect crease.

"Please stay," I say aloud.

—You're young and strong. If you get sick, you'll recover.

—That's what you told Ernestina.

She slaps me hard. —What's happened to you?

A shadow passes over my face. "Who's there?" I ask. No one, just a dust blossom rising from the path and the bloom of three red fingers on my cheek.

*   *   *

Are those the black stars falling? Papà lifts his hands to catch them. He will save us from this black rain. Remember, Papà, that thou art only dust. Come in. Come in. Black stars break against the window. Is it rain? Is it rain? I cannot help myself. I close my eyes.

*   *   *

Ernestina turns in her bed and inhales. The air makes its noisy passage to her lungs. I breathe for both of us, feel her chest narrow with each exhalation. I breathe in again, ignoring the tightness in my own chest.

The rasp of Antonio's scraping carries from the kitchen into our bedroom. He has made his ninety-second mark.

"*Ho sete*, Mamma," Ernestina whispers.

"*Ho sete*, Mamma," I echo.

Later, I will not be able to get the cadence of our pleas and the drumming of the rain against the roof out of my mind, even when I sleep. Much later, I will remember only a melancholy music.

FEVER

"*Ho sete*, Mamma."

No one here to care for me? Ernestina's bed is empty. Has my sister risen from the dead? Surely she'll come back with water from the well.

Somewhere, the click of rosary beads...

"Ernestina? Can it be you?"

Two spokes of the same star, my sister and I. I touch her hair, I touch my hair, our little girls' bodies returned to us.

And here's Mamma by our bed as we lie down to sleep.

—*C'era una volta*, Mamma begins.

—Once upon a time, a mother had two daughters. One was bad, and the other was very, very good. The mother tells the bad daughter, Go! Draw a bucket of water from the well.

"But I'm weak and can't draw the water."

—And so the good daughter goes to the well instead. She doesn't return for the longest time. We despair, the bad daughter and I.

"Is that you, Mamma?"

But Mamma is gone. Faraway, rosary beads click, click, click. Spare my bad daughter, they say.

A wet cloth on my brow to cool this Spanish fever. It's my brother, Antonio, or no, it's *Ernestina* next to me, laughing, her head propped up on my pillow. She speaks to me in her crystal voice.

—The good daughter goes to the well to draw the bucket of cool spring water. But she's clumsy, this good daughter, her hands always shake, and the bucket falls down, down, down into the well. She's afraid to return to Mamma empty-handed. Her sister is dying, and she needs cool water for the wash-cloths and the thirst.

"That's not in the story."

—It's my story to tell.

My sister's voice is a dream of bells.

—And so the good daughter climbs down the well and finds a long passage with three doors. At the first door, she knocks, and a saint answers. She knows it's a saint because of the bright golden halo in his hands. He polishes his halo and puts it on his head and says, Good daughter, I'm sorry, I haven't seen your bucket. So she knocks on the second door, and the devil answers. She knows it's the devil because he has two knobby horns. She asks if he's seen her bucket and the devil replies, If you help me with these horns, you see, they're very painful. But the good daughter knows better than to bargain with the devil.

Ernestina throws back her head and laughs. How is it possible for someone dead to be so beautiful? I touch her, and she breaks in two. I remove my hand slowly and watch as her body knits itself whole.

—And so, the good daughter arrives at the third door. She knocks, though she's given up ever finding her bucket, and she fears she'll be lost forever in this passageway of doors. Lo and behold, who should answer but the Virgin herself? She knows it's the Virgin from her halo, even brighter than the saint's, and the Christ-child Himself sleeping in the corner. The good daughter is so astonished that she forgets all about her missing bucket. The Madonna looks weary, so the good daughter asks, Is there any-thing I can do to help? The Madonna replies, Can you stay with my boy while I visit my cousin Elizabeth? Her son John is quite ill, and I must take fresh water and this chicken soup to her.

"Mamma's chicken soup? With the tiny bits of carrots and onions?"

—The very thing!

Is that Mamma in the corner? Ernestina wrings a fresh

washcloth and wipes my body head to toe, moving slowly as her words move through the air.

—The good daughter agrees to watch over Jesus. She reads to the child and when He cries, she feeds Him the soup but eats none herself. When the Madonna returns, she says, For your kindness, I will reward you. Here's your bucket filled with fresh water. When you reach the end of this passage, go out into the darkness and look up to the sky. So the good daughter takes the bucket and makes her way down the long passageway and into the night. She looks up at the sky and just at that moment, the single bright star falls upon her brow. As she nears home, her mother runs down the road to meet her, saying, Good daughter, where have you been, and who put that star on your forehead? Her mother tries to wash the star away, for it's something she doesn't understand. But the star shines even brighter...

Starlight burns my eyes, then Ernestina is gone, her bed empty, and here's Antonio wringing a washcloth, there's Papà in the corner.

"Where's Mamma?" I ask.

"In the kitchen, praying," Papà says.

Nearby and faraway, the click of rosary beads...

Mamma, I confess, I'm the bad daughter who wished for the same things as her sister. I went to the well for water to cool Ernestina's fever. I went to the well but didn't know saint from devil. I left the bucket and ran up into the night and there were no stars, only blackness, and a piece of that blackness fell onto my forehead.

"Hush," Papà says.

"*Ho sete*, Ernestina," I whisper, but she's gone to the well and won't ever return.

Antonio presses a wet sponge to my lips, sweet relief for this unquenchable thirst. Papà opens his mouth to speak, but it's Mamma I hear, softly murmuring as if in prayer, "Oh Madonna! I have loved the wrong daughter."

FALLING THROUGH
THE NEW WORLD

I. BEFORE

Let's start from the Piazza Michelangelo Merisi da Caravaggio, whose name is longer than the piazza is wide, just a patch of earnest green, and a stone bench where the gossips debate our village Roccamaro's unfolding history, and three spiny blackthorn trees profuse this time of year with delicate white flowers. Let's start here, in front of the church of San Ponziano. Let's greet the toothless gatekeeper who tolls the bell at noon each day, and dusts the Virgin's shrine, and pockets the wedding coins rained down upon each happy couple to safeguard their future. Let's look across the empty square to the Desiderios' home, where Vincenzo Desiderio, my own Vincenzo, grew up. It's the pale bronze stucco house, just there, the one with purple bougainvillea framing the alcoved doorway.

When Vincenzo's mother was alive, she'd sit inside that doorway and read. *The Inferno of Dante, The Tragical History of Dr. Faustus*, all manner of Hell. This caused a minor scandal in our village, even though she found the books in the convent library. She'd read after the midday meal and, in the late afternoon, take her *passeggiata* to the convent down the hill. There, she'd trade that day's book for another. She had a girl come in two days a week to take her laundry and clean the house, for she was a frail woman. No one knew quite what was wrong with her. She didn't even breathe in the normal way.

At least that's what the gossips said. In the morning, she'd kiss her husband good-bye outside their home and kiss hello when he returned at night—two more scandals, for no one but he worked during the long, hot afternoon, and no other couple kissed so passionately hello and good-bye. Signore Desiderio owned the *Grande Magazzino*, as he called it, a store that sold a bit of everything—bolts of cloth from as far away as England, tablecloths and antimacassars, hand-tailored suits and ready-made shirts, Milanese ties and Florentine belts, men's felt hats and ladies' straw ones, church veils that I wove for him on bobbins and pins, and even an exquisite French dress that no one could afford but stood on a dressmaker's dummy in the display window for years, just to lure people into the shop.

Signore Desiderio's four sons, Lelio and Michele, Arturo and Vincenzo, helped run the shop. Lelio was the one who traveled abroad to bring back the store's wonderful oddities. And then all four brothers volunteered together for the Great War. Michele and Arturo were killed at Isonzo. As to Lelio and Vincenzo? We didn't know yet what had become of them.

But that came after. Let me speak of before.

For my sister Ernestina and me, the Desiderios had their allure, the eccentric family with the four handsome brothers who were always quick with a wink, a *ciao, Ernestina, ciao, Annina, le donne più belle di tutto il mondo*. Michele proposed to Ernestina and Vincenzo to me in the chaos of their departure before they shipped out in 1915. Together she and I even made our wedding dresses after their deployment. A blessing Michele would never know that, like him, she died as a result of the war, of the Spanish influenza and not a bullet like one that killed Arturo or the strange gas that seared and sealed Michele's lungs and fate.

How my mind wanders! Let me speak of before.

Before everything changed, we'd go to the *Grande Magazzino* together, Ernestina and I. The shop wasn't far from our small home and olive grove at the bottom of the hill. Sometimes

I'd bring Signore Desiderio a new veil I'd woven to sell in his shop, but always we'd bring him bottles of fresh-pressed virgin oil during autumn, the months of pressing. Papà would cluck his tongue at us, shameless girls, but would nevertheless offer us the dozens he made daily during harvest season. We took six bottles each day, only six. We'd arrive at the shop, breathless, fanning ourselves with our floral fans, even in December. Michele and Vincenzo would give each of us a piece of Ernestina's favorite, vanilla *torrone*, and my favorite, almond *croccante*, from two tall glass jars that held only these candies, the only two they stocked. They had a third jar, always empty, from which they'd pull nothing and hand the bit of nothing to us. And every time we'd ask, "What is this air?" And they'd say, "It's not air! It's *baci*, the finest *baci* in all the world," and they'd hold their hearts where we'd wounded them, and while we were apologizing, every day the same sugar-sweetened apology for our ignorance, they'd bend quickly to touch our hair and steal from each of us a chaste kiss.

I didn't know then that my life had already moved into its after.

Mamma approved of the boys. The Desiderios had the nicest home in the village, save for the rectory, and her girls were not destined for Holy Orders. She envisioned herself someday in that house at the top of the hill. She'd trade the smoke and ash and flies and shadows of our olive grove at the base of the hill for their green shutters and purple bougainvillea, their terrazzo roof and the merciful cool of the cloistered archway, their proximity to San Ponziano and its flickering votive candles, to the Virgin and God. She dreamed of Papà retiring from his life as a part-time olive grower to become a full-time artisan making the finest men's clothes. People—not only from Roccamaro, but also from the neighboring villages—would come and buy their clothes from him.

Yes, when she looked across the piazza each day after Holy Mass at San Ponziano, she imagined a time in the not-too-distant future when frail, frail Signora Desiderio would no longer sit under the flower-laden alcove reading her hellish books. There instead would be Papà propped in the woman's fine ladder-back chair, his baskets primed with notions. My Vincenzo was also a tailor—Signore Desiderio had taught his son before devoting himself to the village's finest shop—yes, each day Mamma could almost see Papà and Vincenzo sitting side by side, making suits to go with the felt hats sold at the *Grande Magazzino*. And that is why she arranged for Ernestina and me to marry our sweethearts in hasty civil ceremonies before they shipped out.

It was in that very archway that I first saw Vincenzo, a boy of six, making castles out of gray thread-cones and wooden spools on the cobblestones near his father's feet. I loved the way he examined each spool and cone and sized up his building to determine how best to lay out the day's castle. On this day of before, one of the spools rolled away from him and began its long journey down the cobbled hill. Without thinking, I chased after it, picking up speed as I ran downhill, until I tripped and fell on top of it. The very next minute, Vincenzo was bending over me, offering his hand and laughing.

Indignantly, I shook my head and cried. My nose ran and my hair fell across my face in a black and tangled veil and he *laughed* at me. I must admit I hated him right then.

He took the spool from my hands and pressed his father's white handkerchief hard on my bloody knee. I remember the pain of his care, and the little scandal of that bare knee.

II. DRECZENCA IS BURNING

I, Vincenzo Desiderio, am a tailor. A *tailor*, not a soldier.

While the mountains burn, I make perfect seams in fine wool, as my father taught me. The thrum of the machine under my fingers reminds me of him. I can't help but wonder about his fate. My Austrian captors tell me he's probably dead. But as I sew, I choose to imagine myself as a boy sitting on my father's lap, bent low over a stretch of black gabardine. The machine's needle drills the fabric we guide along a groove in the needle plate. A solitary fly carves circles just above the machine, mimicking the spin of the spool of linen thread impaled on its metal spike. My father sucks on the stub of an unfiltered cigarette, stretching the smoke sideways, forming crooked O's that rise into blue air and fade away.

The mountains are on fire.

I make perfect seams in winter-weight wool, cassimere and gabardine, the finest cloth, manufactured here by the Viennese. There's an officers' ball this Saturday. The Commandant tells me it'll boost morale.

Someday I'll have to tell my Annina and our children that I made a black evening coat and a white-pleated shirt with ivory buttons while Dreczenca burned. Someday I'll tell them that I was warm and fed well enough, even as the Viennese starved. Someday I'll explain that Caporetto was a bad dream—that we hadn't meant to surrender but only retreat.

How could it be that handfuls of Austrian soldiers kept thousands of Italian prisoners marching meekly two-by-two? True, some of us *were* cowards. Some but not all, as our General Cadorna claimed. We were surrounded, the hills to the south cut off by fire, Dreczenca throwing off red sparks, the bridges blown. So we laid down our rifles and marched.

We marched past an Italian farmer plowing under the golden chaff of winter wheat, his wife hanging sheets in the wind, a chimney puffing smoke. Only after we passed did we see that half of their house was blown away. We crossed the border into Austria. There, the same farmers plowed the same fields, the same smoke curled from the same chimneys, wives hung the same white sheets.

I thought I'd feel myself passing over the dark line separating one country from another, like a finger running over the edge of the *Grande Carta Topografica*, over the raised border to the place where the vineyards and stone cottages dissolved into a haze of indistinct gray. But I felt only snow caking inside my boots, the same hunger and the same cold, day after day.

I didn't hate the Austrian guards who marched with us. They were children, no more than eighteen. Prisoners' clothing or guards' shoes—I repaired them equally with my smuggled needles and thread torn from the uniforms of the dead. I made clothing to keep the living alive. Then the Commandant offered me this warm hut and hot food, beautiful fabric with which to make him fine clothes. Is there something wrong in that?

Annina weaves lace from air. I had a ribbon of it tucked into my helmet. At night, before I fall asleep on my cot, I remember its scent—sweet and pure—like bougainvillea.

The lace is gone, and Annina is a dream.

We're lying on a soft blanket, hidden behind her father's olive grove. We're young, and the burning between us is like the fire on the mountains. Was Dreczenca burning even then?

"Stop," she says, pushing me away with her hand. "We must wait until after we're married in the Church."

And so, the fire cooled. And so, we waited.

III. THE MOURNING VEIL

Come. Let's begin this special veil. We'll start in the upper-left corner and work from left to right, from pin to pin until we reach the lower-right corner. The sooner we begin...

The sooner our grief will end.

Did you say something, Anna?

No, Sister Benedict. I'm ready.

Your mamma wants teardrops on a black ground. A wonderful idea, but complicated. To get a head start, I've pricked the design onto paper and pinned the pattern to this pillow.

Mamma gave me black silk thread. She said, Use only the finest silk. Use only the weaver's knot.

Your mamma's right. Here, let's place the first pins. Be careful, child, you've pierced your finger. Let me stop the bleeding.

Ho sete.

Are you thirsty, child?

No. Did I speak?

Are you ready for the bobbins?

Yes, Sister.

There you go. You're doing beautifully! Now work the weft horizontally left to right. All other threads are passives. Cross-twist, cross-twist. Let go of the pair of bobbins in your left hand. Now transfer the pair in your right hand to your left. That's it. Pick up pair three with your right hand.

Do not go empty-handed. Bring gifts to the friars every day. A gift is a stitch. A stitch is a prayer. A prayer is a bead. A bead is a way to count your suffering.

Are you listening, child? Cross-twist, cross-twist. Pair nine, pair ten.

Your sister...my dear daughter, was so beautiful, even in death, Anna. I dressed her in her wedding dress.

Ernestina's death still doesn't seem real. Sometimes I swear I can hear her voice.

It's a shame you were ill and couldn't attend. It was a lovely funeral.

Do you think Michele was there in heaven to greet her?

I have no doubt. God's will be done. Today we must work. There, you've finished the first row. Good, good. Put a pin in the pinhole. Be careful of your fingers! Now move the weft right to left. Place a pin at that turn. Repeat. Keep the thread tight. Make sure the pattern is even.

I need a new strand of thread.

Make a knot and pin it to the pillow. Even a wrong pull of the knot can spoil your piece.

But the veil is just for mourning.

You'll use it all your life.

Mamma will, you mean.

Does it matter whose is whose? We all wear black veils for

Ernestina. Do you need a break, dear? Some water, maybe?

No thank you, Sister.

Va bene. Let's continue. Keep your palms up. Hold the bobbins straight. The silk's so fine, let's use three twists. *Three* twists, child. Oh dear, let me unwind that mistake. There, there, you're doing fine. Come now, tears, too, will spoil the lace.

I'm thirsty.

Here. A glass of water. Are you all right, child? Put the bobbins down. The lace can wait. Better? The color is returning to your face.

Mamma says I'm recovered well enough from the influenza to mourn. She says I must wear the veil six months, but she must wear it for one year.

She has the greater sadness, child.

She has me every morning weaving bobbins around pins. She says it will pass the time till Vincenzo returns. I sometimes feel as if I'm weaving stitches in my sleep.

Then let's do some easy stitches. A braid. You *could* do this in your sleep. Did you know the French for braid is *bride*? You'll be a bride again when you marry Vincenzo in the Church. That day isn't far off, now is it, child? Ready to *bride*? Let's begin. Cross-twist, cross-twist. Repeat. Spread the bobbins. Keep the braid tight. Here, Anna, let *me* make the weaver's knot this time. See, the threads look like two circles kissing. Let's hide our eyes. It's a joke. Two circles kissing. I made a joke. Ha. Ha. My, you're quiet today, Anna!

Forgive me, Sister. I *am* tired.

Here, child, you've missed this pin.

Why did you become a nun?

I was called to be a bride of Christ.

Did you hear God's voice in the night?

It wasn't like that. It was more a longing.

Why would God take Ernestina and leave Mamma?

Anna! You mustn't think such things. God has a plan for each of us.

He works in silence.

In the silence are His words. And truly six months is such a short time to grieve.

Must I wear the black veil even when I sleep, Papà?

No, Annina, even sadness sleeps.

When I lie down, that's when I cry.

This is the reason for the veil. To hide your tears.

May I become a bride of Christ?

He's already taken. Besides, you married Vincenzo in the town hall before he left. It's how he endures whatever he endures.

Vincenzo is dead.

We don't know that. I'll not listen to such things. Imagine yourself instead a vision in white. Vincenzo at the altar in San Ponziano, waiting for you. They say you're never happier.

A vision in white with a black veil.

You've dropped a bobbin.

The dead bride in her wedding dress.

Now we're ready for the next cross.

We all have our crosses to bear, Anna.

There, there. The tears again. We can finish tomorrow. Postponing mourning another day won't matter. Come here, child. See? See how well the veil already drapes your face?

IV. PRISONER-OF-WAR

Look at Herr Desiderio, they say, in his black tails and starched white shirt, black silk tie and cummerbund, peering through the tall palace windows. Are we not civilized men? Does he not have a suit that compares to the finest livery of the *Feldzeugmeister* and *Kommandantinnen*, to the gowns of our beautiful wives hiding behind their gold fans, to the pearl-and-diamond tiaras worn by our comely daughters? Does he not drink the same champagne as we do, from the same fluted crystal? Does he not dine on smuggled French foie gras and Russian caviar in the Hofburg instead of starving in the camp? Why, then, does he peer through the window rather than join us at the ball?

Does the Italian think he's better than us? It's he who should not be allowed to look upon our daughters. See how he watches the women dancing to the cries of *Walzt! Walzt! Walzt!* Does the dance not take his mind from the troubles of the war for one evening? Does the dance not make him forget his frail mother, worrying Rosary after Rosary over the fate of her four sons, and the gaping hole in the pale bronze stucco of his mountain home left by the *Jagdgeschwader*, and San Ponziano blasted open, the statue of the Madonna and child lying on its side amidst fallen stone? Does the dance not instead recall his parents' kisses, fodder for the gossips' gossip, and his Annina weaving lace for exquisite ball gowns in the shade of bougainvillea?

We celebrate even as our Empire falls in tatters. You see, they say, we're civilized men.

They know he won't run. Where is there to go? And even if he goes there, wherever this *there* is, who'd welcome him? He sees a boy playing with empty thread spools, building castles out of air. Is that the same boy now begging in Stephansplatz? He sees a young woman weaving fabric from air, weaving air into kisses, the finest *baci* in the world. Is that the same woman on the steps of St. Stephen's who now tugs at the legs of passersby, crying for news of her missing husband, reconciling herself to the fate of all widows?

Would this widow dance with me? Would she forget her dead husband if I explained how her fair city seduced me with its private places, its shimmering palaces and jeweled churches?

Annina, *carissima*, I swear I was bewitched by a bead of sweat trickling down the nape of a woman's neck. I can see it there, through the tall palace window, a single bead of sweat, just below her diamond hairpins.

V. AFTER

I've kept my hair exactly as it was before Vincenzo left. How many of us honor the memory of before? There's a spot on my shoulder blade, a black mole the size of a bobbin-head. My hair touched this mole the day he left. When Ernestina was alive, she'd pin up my hair in ten layers and cut each one separately, to this very spot. She said it was like taming the ocean. When she was done, she'd kiss the top of my head.

"*Bellissima*," she'd say, "there's not enough beauty in the world."

We'd talk while she cut, about Vincenzo, or about her dead Michele. "Michele," she'd say, "was far too gentle for the world. That's why he died."

Ernestina, too, was too gentle for the world. And so she left to be with Michele. This is what I tell myself as I wait for Vincenzo at the dock in Pescara where the soldiers return from the war. Vincenzo isn't gentle. He makes his demands, takes what he wants. I know this, and still I love him. Or perhaps because of this I love him. He survived precisely because he's not gentle. I, too, survived because I'm not always gentle or patient or kind.

Yes, he took what he wanted, but my wants had edges—the place where his body crossed over into mine. I said, "Wait." It was Mamma who insisted we wait until the Church conse-crated our union.

I've imagined the moment he'll reach me as I stand among the crowd of women at the dock. He'll gather my hair along the ends and wrap it three times around his fist. Then he'll pull my head back and kiss my neck, just here, in the hollow. The pres-sure of his lips will stop my breath. This is something I haven't forgotten lying alone in my bed for almost four years—three twists and a kiss, that pause in time.

After Ernestina died, Mamma couldn't be bothered with my hair. If I'd given her the scissors, she'd have cut it straight across my back.

"Vanity," she told me when I asked for this modest favor,

"is a bruise you wear inside."

To which I responded by wrapping my hair three times around my fist and pulling so hard a hank tore from its roots. My brother, Antonio, found me crying. He stood behind me, pinned up my hair in exactly ten layers, and cut each layer so that the curls fell just so. All this because I promised myself I wouldn't change.

But how do you create memories that never existed? For almost four years Vincenzo has been gone, years of nothing to hold onto. He shipped out in June 1915, fought in the mountains until he was captured at Caporetto in November 1917, and spent the past year languishing in an Austrian POW camp. I hadn't even received a telegram since before the battles of the Isonzo until the notice came that he was returning home. In the silence of those years, I imagined him counting days with strokes of a sharp stone against concrete while I wove mourning veils.

There he is. Vincenzo. Just another Italian soldier descending the ramp from the boat that disgorges the living and the half-dead and the dead.

You're not thin, you're not pale, you're just the same, I say to myself, denying what I can plainly see.

True, he doesn't come stoop-shouldered or maimed. Some men grasp canes, pretend their missing leg is still there. I can hear their wives gasp. Each husband's hobbled walk from the gangplank to where his wife stands is enough time for her to summon the other woman, the woman who will dust the prosthetic leg and set it in the corner each night, as if it were a piece of furniture or a holy relic, then make love to her husband while pretending his ghost limb is real.

Soldiers with two arms crush their wives to their chests. Those with one arm cling lopsidedly to the women who have already begun to drown. The men without arms depend on their wives to hold them.

Petty as I am, I'll wonder for the rest of my life what it would be like to make love to one of these half-men.

Vincenzo squeezes me with his two good arms until I

can't breathe. His body feels like bones pressed against my ample flesh.

"You look well," I gasp, but he says nothing. I try again. "*Carissimo*, Vincenzo."

"*Indimenticabile*, Annina," he replies. Unforgettable.

These words will do. He imagines, already, my flesh against his.

I've brought my bicycle to the dock. Mamma told me that a lady in a skirt does not ride a bicycle, so I've worn a pair of Antonio's pants under my dress.

"Would you like a ride, soldier?" I say, and sweep my hand over the bicycle at our feet.

He smiles at me, then wraps my hair around his fingers and presses his fist against my back until I wince. He does this, and this alone, and releases me. I'm foolish enough to believe there's still the promise of stop-time.

Righting the bicycle, I straddle the crossbar. He mounts the bicycle behind me and presses his thighs astride my hips. I put my right foot on one pedal and push hard, then lift my left foot and begin a slow circling for the long ride ahead. The bicycle wobbles as I steer around couples holding onto each other, children wiping runny noses, birds scavenging in the dirt.

We're on the verge of falling, always on the verge of falling through the new world. And finally we're free of the crowds, and the bicycle gathers speed down the slope that leads away from the dock. The air lifts my hair into his face. I can feel his breath on the nape of my neck.

Soon, I think, in six hours or six months or six years, we'll be home.

PART II: *ISOLA DELLA SPERANZA,*
ISOLA DELLE LACRIME

PROVIDENCE
(NOVEMBER 1922)

We've traveled all day from Roccamaro in a borrowed truck, my brother, Antonio, at the wheel, tap-tap-tapping incessantly. When we bounce over a particularly rough bump, my husband, Vincenzo, holds his arm across my stomach. Behind us, his trunk dances across the wooden floor of the flatbed, back and forth, as if something alive inside is fighting to escape.

What he's thinking I can only imagine. We've said little to each other since we left home in the morning dark, and Antonio has been silent except for the tapping. The roads, some a spit's width of worn earth rutted with tire treads, cross the narrow band of the heart of Italy from our home to the Naples dock. Bile rises in my throat, and I swallow it.

Vincenzo tears off a corner from the loaf of bread we packed for the journey.

"You must eat, *bella mia*," he says, urging the bread toward my lips. He's been strangely solicitous all day, his sideways glances betraying concern.

I shake my head and press my lips together. I can't eat even a crust of bread.

How do you say good-bye to your husband over and over again? The hardest part isn't that we don't know how long the separation. The hardest part is the parting. Like every parting, I suppose, his arms enclosing me, a kiss on the lips—and then?

"Antonio," I say, pressing my hand on top of his. For several minutes, his hand is blessedly still. Then his fingers begin to quiver, playing over the gearshift. A random pattern of beats erupts—thumb to pinky, pinky to index, index to ring. The rhythm penetrates my chest. My heart feels as if it's beating erratically in time with his fingers. There's no air left to breathe in the cramped quarters of the truck's front seat. I bend over till my head is between my knees. A thin stream of green liquid runs from my mouth.

"Please, Antonio," I say, wiping away the bile. He shoves his hand under his leg.

"Pull over," Vincenzo says. Antonio brings the truck to a stop in the middle of the road. "Come." Vincenzo, already half out of the truck, extends his hand toward me.

I shake my head. "The boat will leave without you."

"The boat will wait for us."

He lies, knowing the boat is an impatient mistress. She doesn't wait for anyone, least of all a second-class passenger and his meager belongings. Climbing back into the seat, he removes his handkerchief from his breast pocket and dampens it with water from a glass bottle we've passed among us since dawn. The well water is warm from a long day in the truck. He presses the wet cloth to my forehead. I lean against him, and the nausea passes. The wet cloth and the heat and the rise and fall of his chest make me sleepy. We could be eighteen again and not thirty with so many years between us. I doze.

*　　*　　*

"Wake up," Vincenzo says, nudging my shoulder.

I wake slowly to seabirds shrieking, babies crying. All around our truck, mothers hold infants aloft as toddlers tug on their wide skirts. *Arrivederci, Papà. Arrivederci, Francesco, Guiseppe. Arrivederci, carissima mia.*

The dock is madness. Everyone is crying, even the workers who load suitcases and trunks and crates on wooden carts and wheel them aboard ship. They're sorry to see anyone leave the *paese*. Whistling an incongruously upbeat tune, Antonio places Vincenzo's battered

38

trunk on one of the carts and disappears into the crowd. As I watch his back fade away, I wonder if he, too, will leave me.

Vincenzo looks at me as if he expects me to tell him something. What would he have me say? It's a relief to see him go? I don't know who he is anymore. Before the war, a hundred years ago, a thousand, he would curl his tongue and touch his nose to make me laugh. I don't remember the last time he made me laugh or the last time he laughed. He wakes at five, dresses in a starched white shirt and perfectly creased pants, and wolfs down a hard roll and black coffee for breakfast. Then it's daily Mass and tailoring by seven, the birds barely begun their trilling. No one in Roccamaro begins work at seven. No one works without pausing.

He's told me of the Viennese, their exceptional work ethic and their conformity. These are the tenets of his new faith. We should become like one another, he says, completely alike. This sameness will prevent another war, he says. I reply, If the Austrians are so superior to us, how come they lost the war? He shakes his head. I say, You want all of us wound up like clocks, spinning through our days? He tells me I don't understand. He's lost hope with us Italians, how we think a working day ends at one, how we argue over which province has the best cuisine, how we look down on our compatriots to the south as if they're a different race. He sees the rise of Mussolini as a warning and can't understand why we don't see it too. He talks as if he's already no longer one of us. I tell him that the stress of war has altered his mind. My mind is fine, he tells me, tapping his head. America, he says, America is one great melting pot. As if that explains everything.

There's no dissuading him. His brother and sister-in-law, Lelio and Theresa, are settled in Philadelphia, so he won't be alone. Lelio has started a tailor shop and has more business than he can handle since he won a contract for men's clothing from a new kind of *Grande Magazzino*, a department store called Wanamaker's.

"Imagine a single store twelve stories tall with a grand hall and a giant bronze eagle in the promenade!" he has told me.

"That's America! I'll earn the money to bring you over on the finest ship, in first class no less. It won't take long."

That's his plan. What's not in his plan: *I am pregnant.*

I should tell him before he leaves, but these three words would lay waste to his carefully constructed future, to everything he's dreamed of.

He takes my chin in his hand, mistaking my silence for sadness. "A year or two isn't terribly long to wait," he says. "You waited longer during the war."

But our child will no longer be an infant, I think.

"There will still be time." He kisses me, once on each cheek, then strides to the edge of the pier, cups a palmful of water, and lets it run between his fingers. "It's the same water in America," he says, drying his hand on his pants leg as he walks back to me.

There are tears in his eyes as he moves his face toward mine. I tilt my head up to meet his lips, a pleasant kiss so unlike those we shared during surreptitious rendezvous when we were engaged. This was before the war. That passion is gone. Mamma says it's to be expected.

"See," Vincenzo says, pointing to the lettering on the side of the ship. "From your arms into the arms of *Providence*." He means it as a joke. I force a smile, and he hugs me as a reward for this small obedience.

Vincenzo kisses me again on both cheeks, then weaves through the crowd toward the ship.

Nothing would have stopped him from leaving, I tell myself, patting my stomach. *Not even the promise of a child.* Too much has been invested in this trip to change plans at the last minute. Besides, there have been almost four years of trying, a miscarriage, so much false hope.

Vincenzo's head appears above the ship's railing, a miniature planet rising from an artificial horizon. He waves, and I return his farewell.

"I'm pregnant," I say out loud, continuing to wave. A young boy next to me looks up. He's clutching both ends of a dowel, which holds a fat spool of white thread, its tail trailing up the gangplank before it disappears into the bowels of the ship.

"I'm pregnant," I say to him. "I'd like to have a son like you."

The boy tugs on his mother's sleeve, his brown eyes never wavering from mine. She bats his hand away as if she were shooing a fly, too busy sobbing and waving and blowing kisses to her husband to mind her son as *Providence* lurches from the dock, belching clouds of black smoke. The stern plies the choppy waters of the Gulf of Naples on its way to the Tyrrhenian Sea. The boy's spool unwinds faster and faster as the boat pulls away.

I imagine the distance between Vincenzo and me as that skein of thread unwinding across a vast blue-black emptiness. Just then, the boy's skein breaks before the thread runs out. He begins to cry, and his mother lifts him up into her arms.

"Wave to Papà," she says, and rubs his back.

He throws the wooden spool into the water and wipes his tears with the edge of his sleeve. I watch the spool catch the weight of water and sink. The sea closes over the space.

Antonio materializes beside me like the ghost he's been for several years, inserting himself between spaces in air.

I lean my head into his shoulder. "I'll never see Vincenzo again."

He runs his fingers through my hair to comfort me as *Providence* disappears over the wide rim of the dark sea.

"I'll never see Vincenzo again," I repeat.

He stops stroking my hair. "Impossible," he says, "you're pregnant."

These are the only words he's said all day, a secret we've kept from each other without even knowing.

"It doesn't matter," I say to him.

I disentangle his hand from my hair and walk to the edge of the dock. My finger has swollen slightly around my wedding ring, another sign Vincenzo missed. I dip my hand in the water and tug off the stubborn band. It leaves a red circle around my ring finger. I wonder idly how long the mark will take to fade. A year? Two? I throw the thin gold band into the gulf exactly where Vincenzo scooped the American water, exactly where the thread disappeared.

HO FAME

Luca turns to me and whispers, "*Ho fame*, Mamma."

My son knows that I always keep a little something in my pocket, a piece of soft *torrone* studded with roasted almonds or a bar of the bittersweet chocolate Papà insists on spoiling him with, the expensive Swiss chocolate that's the only one good enough for his grandson.

I give Luca a square of chocolate, which he eats, then another, which he cups in his hand. The chocolate melts on his fingers under the photographer's hot studio lights and stains his new white suit, the one I made just for this photograph to commemorate his upcoming fourth birthday and to send to his father in America. I imagine the moment two years hence when our son will run down the gangplank of the ship that carries us from Naples to New York. He'll fling out his arms, and Vincenzo will scoop him up and press him to his chest.

"*Bambino*," his father will say, then realizing his error, "*mio figlio*."

How easily the reunion forms in my mind when I'm happy!

"*È tempo!*" Signore Fratelli says.

I lift up Luca, and we turn to the camera. The photographer's face is buried beneath the winding black cloth, his legs braced on either side of the tripod. His patent leather shoes reflect the glare of the studio lights as he raises his fist above the camera and says, "*Guardate qui!*"

Luca is frightened. Perhaps it's the large box that's swallowed the man's head and threatens to engulf his shoulders. Perhaps it's his exhaustion from the two-hour journey from Roccamaro to Chieti. It's past his nap time. He begins to cry.

"Hush," I tell him, stroking his back.

"Mamma," he says, and buries his face in my neck.

I know what I'll write to Vincenzo on the back of the photograph—*you're forgetting me*. I haven't seen him in almost five years—won't see him for two more? never?—and everything will be fine once I'm settled in America. Vincenzo will learn to love me again, just as he's learned to love his new *paese*, replacing the love he had for Roccamaro, his stuccoed home at the top of the hill, and the solid, straight-backed chairs in the doorway. I can almost see our brick-faced row home on a quiet Philadelphia street, the three of us rocking on the front porch. The picture wavers at the edges of my vision until all that's left is the gauzy fabric of a dream.

Luca drapes his arms around my shoulders, leaving a tiny thumbprint of chocolate on my new dress. It's warm where he's touched me. I rub at the chocolate, thinking to wipe it away. His thumbprint dissolves into the pattern of my dress. The ache that fills me at night fills me now. Why? Luca is here. He's all I need.

"*Guardate qui!*" Signore Fratelli says again.

I lift Luca's chin, kiss him, and turn his face to the camera.

The bulb flares. In my temporary blindness, I don't notice the pale ghost on Luca's cheek, a reflection of the camera's flash. It's the ghost I'll try and fail to erase forever.

POST CARD
UNITED STATES POSTAGE
AIR MAIL
10
CENTS
10
CORRESPONDENCE
ADDRESS
8 June 1927   Philadelphia
Carissima Annina,

How could we have known Mussolini would
separate us for seven years when I left? I
count the days till the moment when you
and Luca join me. The photograph you sent
shows me I've already missed so much of
his childhood.

Thank God for Lelio and Theresa, or I don't
know if I could bear the loneliness. No, I
haven't forgotten you. Sei indimenticabile!
Saluti infiniti e baci di amore,

        Amo, amo, tuo Vincenzo

Gentile Annina Desiderio
Roccamaro, Italy

LA MANTIGLIA

I remember everything.

*   *   *

Luca is crying. What harm is there in a little lie to soothe my son's tears? His fourth birthday is a week away, but I rely on a child's comprehension of time.

"It's a birthday party for you," I tell him as we walk down the hill of Via Condotti to the outskirts of Roccamaro with my mother. From there his *nonna* will walk him up the neighboring hill to the lake and the picnic that's been planned to celebrate the feast of Saint Veronica, the saint who wiped the face of Jesus on His road to crucifixion.

"You spoil him," Mamma says. "He goes to the lake because you say he goes. He goes because you have work to do. You work so you can buy him a tricycle, and not just any tricycle, but the best tricycle money can buy. No secondhand tricycle for my grandson."

I let her talk. What's the good of contradicting her? I turn my back on her even before she finishes her sentence, but her words have the odd effect of comforting Luca. She's inadvertently reminded him that for his fourth birthday, he'll get the black tricycle that's hanging in the shop window across the cobbled street from where we stand. A wooden boy, clothed in white knickers and a white shirt just like my Luca, straddles the tricycle's seat and grasps its handlebars. His face is painted with perfectly round, deep brown circles for eyes and lips red and

O-shaped, so that the mannequin wears an expression of perpetual astonishment. He's been frozen in that position for a year, waiting for someone to wrest the tricycle from his grip. Luca follows my gaze to the window display, and his tears stop. If I don't buy the tricycle, Nonna will. I kiss him on the top of his head and bend to wipe the tears from his cheeks with my apron.

"I must finish the bride's *mantiglia*," I say to him as we continue to gaze at the wooden boy behind the glass. "What would a bride be without her wedding veil? Or her gown?" I pinch his nose. "You wouldn't want to see a naked bride walking down the aisle of San Ponziano, would you, Luca dear?"

He laughs and rubs his nose.

"That's scandalous!" Mamma says. "Putting such ideas in the boy's head!"

"Oh, Mamma, he's only four."

"That's why men are the way they are—because of their mothers!"

"You would know."

It's a terrible thing to say. Her only son, Antonio, was damaged by the war and not by her.

I place a light jacket around Luca's shoulders and squat in front of him. "Wear this. It'll be cool by the lake." He nods solemnly, and I kiss him again.

"Please don't let him wade too far in," I tell Mamma. "And make sure he takes off his stockings and shoes before he wades in the water."

"He's wearing his best shoes to the lake?"

"You're wearing your best dress to the lake?"

"Two pairs? Three pairs? My daughter, such a rich woman. Three pairs of shoes for a three-year-old."

"Mano is a cobbler."

"Mano, Mano. What about Vincenzo?"

"*Per l'amore di Dio!* Mano's my cousin."

Mamma and Luca turn from me and make their way up the stony path that leads to the lake. He glances over his shoulder, and I wave to him one last time.

*　　*　　*

I remember everything about that day.

*　　*　　*

Turning away from the shopkeeper's window, I pass our former home at the bottom of Via Condotti with its now-barren olive grove. Alberto and Marie live there. Rumor has it that Marie is pregnant with their fifth child. Rumor has it that Alberto has a wandering eye for Mamma. I try to imagine them together, Mamma and Alberto. They'll be at the lake with the whole town watching. Let them see what they can get away with, two dozen pairs of eyes searching for a single, careless hand.

Walking uphill, I pause midway at the town's small shrine, a square post crowned by a wooden alcove within which is a cross of the crucified Christ. Mamma says it's a miracle that His wounds shine bright red even after years of bleaching in the sun. I touch His face and think of Veronica's compassionate act, the one we celebrate on this day. According to some, her sacred veil is preserved not far from Roccamaro, in the Basilica Volto Santo di Manoppello. Each year since the cloth was first displayed for public adoration, our family has made a pilgrimage there. Papà drives us in a borrowed truck to the bottom of the steep and winding Via Cappuccini and together we walk uphill, stopping to say Rosaries at each of the wayside shrines that mark the fourteen Stations of the Cross. When we reach the top of the hill and enter the church, we make our way to the altar upon which the veil is displayed, framed between sheets of glass and surrounded by an ornate gilt frame. The countenance of the Holy Face—serene, relaxed—reflects the very opposite of the suffering Jesus experienced as He carried His cross on the way to Calvary. Rather, His eyes are open, His lips slightly parted, as if He wants to tell us something. For her part, Mamma sees only the echo of swelling on the right side of His face and a rust-colored patch that she swears is proof of a bloody wound.

She touches the glass, bows her head, and prays,

> Your face, Lord, I seek.
> Do not hide Your face from me.
> Do not reject Your servant with anger.
> You are my help, do not forsake me,
> God of my salvation.

Always, tears fall from her cheeks as she murmurs these words, as if she's the one who carried the cross to Calvary.

What possesses me to dawdle at Roccamaro's shrine, thinking of Jesus' great sacrifice of the Crucifixion, when Papà is waiting? I bless myself and hurry up the hill, cross the tiny triangle of green with its three blackthorn trees teeming with green berries that will soon ripen to purple-blue. The town's three gossips, dressed in identical pink-flowered housecoats, sit on a stone bench beneath the blackthorns. Silence descends as I pass by. I keep my head down to discourage conversation, but I can hear them.

"How long has Vincenzo been in America?" Concetta asks.

"Five years is it?" Justina suggests.

"A man shouldn't be so long separated from his family if you ask me," Bianca says.

Who asked you? I want to say. They carry on as I cross the square. I only hear bits and pieces of today's conversation, but I've heard it all before. *Anna got the best of that deal after Signore Desiderio died of a broken heart. Yes, and so soon after his frail wife's death! The nicest home in town for her mamma.* As if I planned for Vincenzo's parents to die and two of his brothers to be killed in the Great War and his brother Lelio to leave for America. *Such tragedy to befall such a wonderful family.* As if losing my sister to the Spanish influenza and my brother's mind to the same Great War weren't equally tragic. *A lot can happen in two more years.* As if it were my choice to be separated from Vincenzo for seven long years waiting out Il Duce's harsh mandate that keeps spouses apart for the money husbands send back to their wives. *And sacrilege! Anna and her father working so hard on this blessed feast day!*

Cluck, cluck, cluck, three fat hens, they whisper such things in the shade of San Ponziano. The church traces its long, early morning shadow across the square, capturing the gossips and me in its darkness. I follow the steeple shadow away from them, treading on the edge where shade meets sunlight, to the doorway of Vincenzo's family home, *our* home, where Papà sits already hard at work on the groom's suit. The pale bronze stucco surrounding him is bleached even paler by the morning sun, and the dark green shutters gleam. The gossips are right about one thing—Mamma traded me for this home. Yes, I can be cruel, especially when cruelty is two parts suffering. The truth is, I *wanted* to marry Vincenzo, and Mamma and Papà and Antonio only moved in with us *after* Signore Desiderio's funeral, a few months before Vincenzo left for America.

"Good morning, Papà," I say, and kiss the top of his head.

Papà brushes cigarette ash from the black serge morning coat he's making for the bridegroom. "A perfect day, no?" he says.

"Luca's gone."

"So it's not a perfect day." On a small wooden table, he helps me arrange my lace-making notions—the cylindrical pillow upon which the bride's *mantiglia* is evolving with dozens of wooden bobbins dangling from the lace, spools of silk thread and trays of pins close at hand, and a shallow stand on which to rest the pillow when I tire of weaving.

I pick up a pair of bobbins and resume where I left off yesterday, twisting and crossing the bobbins, guiding them along the pins that outline the paper pattern underneath the lace. Row after row of stitches, repeating and repeating, create the delicate mesh of the wedding veil. A single bird with two heads facing away from each other rises out of nowhere, floats in the airy ground, and dissolves at the edges. *Fond à la vierge*, the pattern is called. The bride found the pattern in a French catalogue of women's wedding finery, the veil fashioned after the Spanish *mantilla*. Since the war, we've all become Europeans.

Fond à la vierge. I must admit it's stunning.

The silk thread wears maroon ridges in my fingers, but trifles like cuts and blisters don't matter. The bride will be pleased. Women from as far away as Pescara, the big city, order their wedding dresses and veils from me. They've heard of the smoothness of my lace. They don't know my secret: knots, even fine ones, spoil the material. Here are my three simple rules: Start with long threads. Keep the bobbins straight. Work in an uninterrupted flow. Some knots are unavoidable—those joining a new length of thread to an existing one when the bobbin runs out. Those I tie off only with the weaver's knot. It's stronger, less likely to unravel, and smoother, though it's time-consuming to make.

Mamma tells me that I'm too particular even though she insists I use the weaver's knot for *her* lace. "What do these peasants know?" she asks as she eats the bread their lace puts on our table.

"What's the matter?" Papà asks. With a needle and thread, he's basting one of the black satin lapels to the body of the groom's morning coat to hold it in place for the sewing machine. A cigarette composed mostly of ash dangles from his mouth.

"I was just thinking how impossible Mamma is."

"Someday you'll miss your mother."

"You'll miss me when I'm dead," I say, mimicking Mamma's inflection, her wagging finger.

"See," Papà says. "You two are exactly alike. Your mother means well. She just doesn't know when to stop."

"It's more than that. You of all people should know it."

"You forget she's also suffered."

I suppose Papà is right, but I'm reduced to tallying our losses, as if suffering is something measurable, like lengths of thread. One: Papà has never left Mamma's side, whereas Vincenzo and I have been separated for most of our marriage. Two: I cared for Ernestina when she was dying while Mamma said her Rosaries and made her useless pilgrimages along the Madonna path to the friary. Three: I keep Antonio safe while she laments what she calls his "disabilities." Four: She thinks she's earned the right to leisure while I blister my hands weaving lace.

I make an invisible knot and sigh.

"What's troubling you?" Papà asks.

I want to say "You're wrong, Papà," but I hold my tongue. He doesn't deserve my anger.

He chews on the stub of his spent cigarette, no longer looking at me. I wonder what he remembers, if he remembers only selectively the death of his oldest daughter. Perhaps that's the gift age confers, a smoothing of edges. *Per piacere, Mamma, l'acqua.* There *is* no water and then there's too much.

*   *   *

What I don't remember, I can easily imagine.

*   *   *

Mamma clucks her tongue at Luca as she removes his white jacket and his leather shoes. —*O Dio*, what are we going to do about your mother? Go, go!

She pushes him toward the older children and watches him catch up to them, then remembers she forgot to take off his stockings and to warn him about the lake. *The older children will look after him*, she thinks, turning to Alberto.

—Luca is fat, she says.

Yes, that's what she says, sitting next to Alberto on a blanket in the cool shade of a weeping willow.

Alberto has two sons, which gives him the right to say with authority, —Luca is a baby. Luigi had the same chubby legs when he was three. Now my Marie's worried he doesn't eat enough.

—I've raised a son, and I say he's fat. She folds Luca's jacket and places it under her head like a pillow.

Alberto knows better than to argue with her. Instead, they watch silently as the children run along the shore, their parents barefoot, talking and laughing and following close behind.

The air skids across the lake and becomes a pleasant breeze, but Luca is hot from his exertions. Beads of perspiration dot his forehead. He passes by the adults and chases after the other children, who tease him with their cries of *Fat boy! Fatherless boy!* They don't wait for him to catch up. Soon his short legs tire of the two steps he takes for each one of theirs. He sits on the shore and removes his soiled stockings. The wet sand feels pleasantly cool oozing between his bare toes.

As the grown-ups pass by, Marie bends to pat Luca's head. —You stay right here, she says. — We'll pick you up on our way back.

He nods. Alone, he catches his breath as he surveys the wide lake rippling in the breeze and the sun glinting off the water.

With her hand, Mamma shades her eyes against the glare, but she can no longer see any of the picnickers. She assumes Luca is with them.

Turning away from the lake, she rolls on her side to face Alberto and spreads the folds of her new dress across the blanket. The dress has a wide lace collar, months and months of my bobbins and pins. She knows the collar's V shape and cream color flatter her narrow shoulders and accentuate her skin tone. Not the darker shade of the Abruzzesi, of me and Papà, but the fair hue of her Spoletini. *I'm still a young woman*, she thinks. *I've taken care of myself.*

Alberto smiles at her, then whispers a crude joke in her ear.

*   *   *

The sun has fallen lower in the sky, hovers above the cap of the tallest neighboring mountain peak. I guess that it must be nearing four o'clock. The day's been hot, even for July, and the falling sun doesn't promise cooling. Oblivious to the heat, Papà pushes the sewing machine's treadle as fast as it will go, the needle plunging up and down through a thick seam. Another cigarette dangles from his lips, and it makes me even hotter to watch the cigarette smoke and redden as he sucks on the unfiltered end. Perspiration beading on my temples threatens to spoil the lace. I pause to dab the sweat with my apron, thinking of Luca, the wide, cool lake, the enticement of water.

"Oh, Vincenzo, Vincenzo," Papà says in a high-pitched woman's voice, sharp lines of smoke spewing from the corners of his mouth. He laughs at his own breathless imitation, a laugh that turns into a fit of coughing. When the coughing dies away, he says, "*O Dio*, I must give up this filthy habit."

As if to prove the point, he stubs out the half-smoked cigarette.

"For your information, I wasn't thinking of Vincenzo. Only Luca."

"He'll be home soon."

Why can't I stop thinking of water? It's the lace I need to concentrate on. Where was I? Two twists and a cross? Two crosses and a twist? I pull hard on one of the bobbins, and a thread breaks. *An extra knot*, I scold myself, absent-mindedly hitting my hand.

"You could start over," Papà says. He's been staring at me, I realize, studying my face.

Not meaning any harm, I toss an empty bobbin at him. It glances off his right cheek and falls to the ground, skipping across the cobblestones. A pinprick of blood boils from the surface of his skin. "Oh, I'm sorry. I was only—"

"This, this is nothing." He presses his finger on the wound. "Why don't you go up to the lake?"

"I can't." I can feel tears stinging my throat and swallow hard. "I can't."

It would be so easy to abandon the bride's veil. I reach in my apron pocket and take out the picture-postcard my husband sent me. On the front is a photo of him and Lelio. The postcard is already dog-eared and covered with fingerprints, Luca's and mine.

Papà snatches the postcard from my hand and stretches back in his chair. He flips the card over and reads, "*Sei indimenticabile*." He smiles. "You may be unforgettable, but your husband is beginning to lose that thick hair."

"Shall I throw something else at you? The pin cushion, or the scissors?"

"That's a beautiful suit," he says, half to himself, running his fingers over my husband's image. "New shoes. A gold tie pin. And didn't you tell me he has a car?"

"A Model T."

"The two of them—they're doing well for themselves with that tailoring business."

"He writes me that they drive through the neighborhood waving to people, who gather to wave back."

"*Principe Lelio, principe Vincenzo.*" He bows to me, his nose practically touching the street. "*Principessa Anna.*" I can't help but giggle.

Pleased to see me laughing, he hands back the postcard and bends to his work.

I'm grateful Papà hasn't noticed Vincenzo's missing wedding ring, or if he has, he's considerate enough not to mention it. I wonder if Vincenzo threw his ring into the sea after mine as his ship hauled itself toward the Mediterranean Sea on its way to New York. Husband and wife, our rings disappearing together into the dark water. I don't know what possessed me to do it. I've had to lie to everyone that I mislaid it. Only Antonio knows the truth. He was there.

What I haven't told Papà is what my husband wrote me in his last letter. *Theresina has been so caring. Theresina brings me wonderful casseroles, almost as good as yours. Theresina keeps me company while I eat. The house is so lonely without you.*

I shake my head, tuck the postcard into my apron pocket, and sigh.

"Just two years more till you join Vincenzo," Papà says. "And two more years we get to spend together before I lose you." Forgetting the vow he made just minutes ago, he lights a fresh cigarette and takes a long drag.

How can I tell my father the truth? That the end started in the

Austrian cell when Vincenzo began to imagine a different life for himself, a life that couldn't be contained by this little village in a country that's all I know. How can I tell him what I've been feeling of late, that Vincenzo and I will never be together? My family, the three of us, fails to form a picture in my head. Why are these images that should be so clear merely gray and shadow?

At four o'clock, the church bells peal the afternoon carillon. I look across to San Ponziano's large red doors, closed now against the sun. The doors swing open, and a young couple emerges from beneath a canopy of hands. The bride and groom hook arms and begin the traditional procession through town. House doors open, one after another.

Felicitazioni, Anna!

Felicitazioni, Vincenzo!

Che tu possa avere molti figli!

The crowd presses lire into the bride's hand as she passes each doorway, which she slips into her wedding purse. She turns to face me. How young she is! How fortunate! Why is it that only then I notice that her veil is black?

* * *

There are things that aren't mine to remember.

* * *

Strange thoughts come to me at night. They're why the shadows never resolve into pictures. I believe there is a God, but He isn't the God of my mother, who sees His hand in all things, who claims to hear His voice. For me, He's a God who works in silence. A God who permits His only Son to carry a heavy wooden cross upon which to be crucified. A God who permits the childish knock on the door. See, there's my sister-in-law, Theresa, Lelio's wife, at my husband's front door, a hot *timballo* in her hands, red gravy bubbling over the edges of the casserole dish. Just that morning she hand-picked the fresh cream mozzarella from the cheese man's cart in the alley behind her house, cut the fettuccine with the strings of the *chitarra*, and rolled the meatballs thick with parsley and garlic and water-softened chunks of stale Italian bread, the way my husband likes them.

He welcomes Theresa with a single kiss on the cheek. A chaste kiss. An American kiss. Her deep brown hair is gathered up loosely with hairpins on the crown of her head. She wears a plain mail-order dress, a blue shirtwaist of the sort women wear in America. Her breasts push up through the thin fabric, the hint of them high and round at her unbuttoned neckline adorned with a simple gold cross. A plain cross—no crucified Christ hanging upon it. She doesn't want to be reminded of suffering.

She passes through the living room and makes herself at home in what will someday be *my* kitchen. From the glass-doored hutch in her borrowed home, she takes down white china plates and bowls, wine glasses, a starched tablecloth, a porcelain bud vase, a silver candlestick. She lights the candle, inserts in the vase a single daisy cut from her window box, fluffs the petals.

—*Vieni*, she says, and pours two glasses of chianti. —*Mangiamo.*

She hasn't forgotten her Italian, I see. She watches him lift a forkful of fettuccine dripping with strings of melted mozzarella to his mouth and savor the pasta with his eyes closed.

—*Delizioso*, he says, and takes another large mouthful. —*Mangia, mangia.*

—*Ho mangiato*, she says, with Lelio and the kids. She must think then of her children and of her husband, no? She doesn't know suffering, hasn't made its acquaintance yet, though she will. Everybody does, sooner or later. She swirls the chianti in her wine glass, takes a long swallow, looks at Vincenzo through the red fingers of wine that stain the bowl of the glass. Ten years younger than Lelio, her brother-in-law is trim, with wavy black hair and transparent blue eyes, a startling combination that never fails to surprise her. Lelio has lost most of his hair. What's left is gray, yellowed at the edges from twenty years of nicotine. His stomach pulls at the buttons of his shirts.

—More, Theresina? he asks. Little Theresa. He holds up the bottle of wine, pours her another glass, and refreshes his.

—A toast, he says, to company. They clink glasses, let them linger together until the ringing dies. They sip in silence until the glasses are drained for a second time. Then he pushes his plate away and brushes crumbs from the tablecloth into his cupped hand. Retrieving a pack of Camels from his shirt pocket, he taps the top of the pack on the table and offers her a cigarette. Lelio forbids it, so of course she takes one, leans into the flame of my husband's lighter, inhaling until the cigarette sparks and burns. He reaches across the table and wipes a fleck of tobacco from the edge of her lip.

—*Grazie mille*, Theresa says. She hasn't forgotten her manners. She's the perfect hostess. She's the perfect guest.

She stays to scrub the crusted gravy from the casserole dish, putting all of her body into the effort. Vincenzo sits at the kitchen table not three feet from her, glancing over the folds of *Il Progresso*, occasionally sharing a bit of news she might find amusing. Through the thin shirtwaist, he can see the outline of her hips, narrower than mine, delicately curved, moving in rhythm to her arms. More of her hair has fallen out of the hairpins. Perspiration beads under her hairline and trails slowly down the nape of her neck, collecting in a dark stain at the collar. She pushes back a strand of hair that has fallen into her face. The slim gold wedding band on her left ring finger reflects the bright light of the ceiling fixture.

He crosses to where she's standing, inhales the sweet undertones of ripe tomato in the gravy that's scented her clothes, and circles her waist with his arms.

* * *

I imagine that's how Theresa cures the hunger of Vincenzo's loneliness.

*　　*　　*

I'm worried about Luca. It's well after six, and I can't concentrate on the lace. The stitches blend together. My index finger begins to bleed from a shallow cut where the thread has worn away the skin. I stop my weaving, not wanting to soil the lace with blood.

"What's the matter, Annina?" Papà asks. "There's plenty of light."

"It's not the light," I say, holding up my wounded finger and stifling a sob.

He pats my hand, then breathes in suddenly, pressing his fingers into his rib cage. The cigarette he was smoking falls to the ground. "*Madre...di...Dio.*" His words come out singly, one for each stuttered breath.

"Papà? Papà!"

He bends over his sewing machine, still pressing his fingers into his rib cage. His breathing is rapid, shallow. A faint whistle comes from his throat.

I rub the space between his shoulders. "I was feeling sorry for myself. That's all. It's nothing. Look at me."

"Just old age," he finally manages to say. He straightens up, wincing. "*Va bene.*"

His right hand trembles as he tries to align a seam along the needle plate's grooved line.

"You work too hard. Rest, Papà. Rest a while and just keep me company. See, the bleeding has stopped," I say, holding up my finger again as evidence.

"I'm fine," he says. To prove the point, he secures the seam between the sewing machine's presser foot and feed dogs, pulls down the clamp, and pushes the treadle with both his feet as fast as it will go. "I'm fine," he repeats over the hum of the machine. "Besides, we can't have both the bride and the groom walking naked down the aisle, now can we?"

"It would give those cackling hens"—I gesture toward the

empty stone bench in the square—"something interesting to talk about. Oh look, there's Luigi."

Coming up the steep hill of Via Condotti, the boy stands on his bicycle pedals, pumping hard as he makes his way toward us. I thank my silent God for Alberto's son. I'll admit I thanked Him then.

*　*　*

Mamma tells me what she chooses to remember. Everything else I must imagine. I don't know the difference anymore between memory and imagination. They're both, in their own way, as real as twin-headed birds woven into lace.

*　*　*

Luca squeezes the mud between his toes as he wades into the water. He splashes the water on his face and feels cooler still. *When will supper be served,* he wonders, *and cake and something to drink? Didn't Mamma say it's my birthday?*

Nonna hasn't even begun to think about eating, only of Alberto's smile and his deep brown eyes and the adults away for the moment.

Luca wades farther into the lake, the water up to his ankles, his knees. The mud sucks at his feet.

Alberto flicks a biting fly from Mamma's neck. She squeezes the flesh to force the poison out. A drop of blood leaks from the swelling flesh and stains her lace collar.

Luca walks in the shallows using the shoreline as a guide, right past Nonna and Alberto, who are too preoccupied to notice. He keeps wading, enjoying the way the water flows past his knees, creating little whirlpools. The water becomes suddenly deeper, up to his hips, yet he continues, the gentle waves lapping his stomach. Thirsty, he bends to the water to have a drink. The water refreshes him, so he drinks again and again. The coolness in his mouth travels down his throat and into his stomach. Then he dips his head under to soothe his whole body.

Marie returns to the place where the picnickers have pitched their camp. She stares at her husband, her fisted hands resting on her wide hips, her belly already casting its own separate shadow. She stands silently, like God, while Mamma and Alberto lean their heads together and laugh. Alberto looks up first, then Mamma, who rises to her knees to face Alberto's wife.

—Luca is missing, Marie says.

Three simple words.

"I couldn't move, you have to believe." That's what Mamma told me. "My legs were rooted to the blanket by the weight of my knees."

I don't believe her, and yet I do believe her.

Alberto calls to his oldest son. —Luigi! *Vieni qui!*

Luigi obeys instantly. He tells his son, —Take your bike. Tell Anna that Luca's missing. *Sprigati, sprigati!*

And so Luigi hastens home, and that's why he arrives alone at the bottom of Via Condotti, straining at his bike pedals.

The picnic becomes a search party. The first things they find are Luca's stockings draped over a fallen tree branch near the shore. Marie picks up the stockings and looks out on the water but sees nothing. The older boys and men wade into the lake, diving and surfacing and diving again. The women and young girls fall to their knees and pray. Mamma, already on her knees, also prays.

I don't know that I'm supposed to be praying, so I don't pray. Instead I watch Luigi pump the bicycle pedals. I see, briefly, in the corner of my eye a vision of my six-year-old Luca, no longer a toddler, running down the gangplank of our ship, leaping into his father's outstretched arms. *The rest can't be far behind*, I tell myself. *Luigi is simply the first.*

*　　*　　*

This is the scene that I have trouble remembering. It's the

scene that blurs together with my imagining Vincenzo and Theresa in America. The two events don't happen on the same day, to be sure. God composes His plan in silence, but He's not quite that methodical. He doesn't always arrange for all one's sorrows to occur on the same day. That's not how suffering works. It's spread over time, or it isn't suffering. When all sorrow is counted in a single day, *that* is tragedy. So we have our tragedies, and we have our suffering. The shell that fell in the trench and killed Antonio's best friend and seared my brother's lungs and damaged his mind, *that* is tragedy. The Austrian Commandant who had my Vincenzo make clothes by day from the finest wool while at night he shivered in a cold cell through his long captivity, *that* is suffering. The blue waters of the lake swallowing a boy and not spitting him back, *that* is tragedy. But, as I said, we weren't to endure a tragedy that day. Instead, God decided to make us suffer.

*　　*　　*

Mamma kneels on the blanket, her head down, clutching Luca's jacket. She prays the Glorious Mysteries of the Rosary, her fingers counting the Hail Marys. How convenient that God has blessed us with ten fingers! In the middle of the fourth mystery, a shadow falls over the blanket. She looks up, expecting divine intervention. A visitation from the Virgin to such a devout woman?

Her eyes follow the shadow to Luca, standing wet and shivering in his muddied white knickers. She rises, staggers on her locked legs, and collapses again to her knees, smothering him with her arms and body, swaying in place as if overcome by the sight of my son.

The search party, completing their circuit of the lake, find the two together. Marie separates herself from the group, extends Luca's muddy stockings, and drops them beside Mamma. Walking back to Alberto, she places her arm around his shoulder. Luca looks from one adult to the next, who blacken the falling sun. He wonders when the party will begin, when food will be served, what flavor the cake, for isn't it his birthday?

*   *   *

Running down the gangplank in America, Luca's almost reached his father's outstretched arms.

*   *   *

Luigi has almost reached the alcove in which we work. Startled by Luigi's strangled cry—"*Signora, Signora*"—I rise up suddenly, knocking sideways the table that holds my lace-making notions. The pillow careens off the table and falls to the ground, the bobbins bounce on the cobblestones, threads wind around each other, hopelessly tangling. The twisting bobbins wrench pins from the pattern, and the lace unravels as if in slow motion. One head of the two-headed bird dissolves into a tangle of thread and air. A week's work gone in a single breath.

Papà urges me forward. "Go on. I'll take care of this."

The lace spoiled, I bless myself, ask God for His help. I'll have to work on Sundays. I promise to offer the work in His name. I begin a quick Our Father, but Luigi's words seal *Thy will be done* forever in my throat.

"Luca's missing," he says, his face flushed red by his bicycling and the sun.

Though it's still summer-hot, his words make me shiver.

I shudder even though I haven't yet heard Luca's moaning as typhoid spreads through his fevered body, slatted shutters drawn against the sun. Nor the timbre of two voices—Ernestina's and Luca's—blending into a single cry of thirst. Nor the click of Mamma's rosary beads at three in the morning, her incantation of the Rosary's great mysteries, the dry rumble of prayer coming from the room next door.

Terrified of catching typhoid, she says she can't help me

63

but for her prayers.

"Someone has to stay well," she tells me. It's a hiccup in time, the very same rosary beads on which she counted her Our Fathers and Hail Marys while Ernestina lay dying.

Her words leave me speechless. My words come later, blue scratches on faintly lined paper.

August 10, 1927

Dear Vincenzo. The fountain pen blots the thin parchment with dark blue stains. I try three simple words. *I love you.* I try three more. *Luca is dead.*

I write these words even though I don't yet know the shadow over Vincenzo's eyes as I walk alone down the gangplank of the ship that brings me to New York. I don't yet know the purity of love for a child, the purity of hatred for a mother. I don't yet know the hundred other unfinished edges of our life.

All I know right then, all that I remember thinking while looking at Luigi's fevered face, is that the wedding is four weeks away, and only a miracle will save the bride's *mantiglia.*

THE PHOTOGRAPH ON THE MANTEL

I hold two photographs side by side. The first, your Uncle Lelio and I resplendent in our summer seersuckers at the photographer's studio in downtown Philadelphia. The other, your mother, my Annina, with you in her arms at a studio in Chieti, chocolate circling your mouth and smeared on her dress.

Luca Desiderio. Who were you, of my blood and bone, not even the whisper of a smile on your lips? Had you somehow known your fate? A ghost on your cheek even then? How didn't I notice it before your death?

I've thought of you in my dreams, holding your arms out to me as you run down the gangplank toward your flesh-and-blood Papà, not the sepia Papà you saw in photographs I sent to your mamma. Papà decked out in his white summer suit, a blue silk handkerchief peeking from his breast pocket and a straw hat tucked under his arm. Papà playing *scopa* with Lelio and his friends on a Saturday night, holding three cards close to his chest, a lone knave of clubs face up on the table. Papà posing in the mountains near the Italian front, fur lining the collar and cuffs of his heavy woolen coat, a revolver in one hand and a walking stick crowned with an M15 helmet in the other. Photographs no doubt creased by the weight of your head on the pillow under which you kept the mementos for safekeeping.

If it weren't for the photograph of you and your mother that I hold in my hands, you'd be forgotten. This photograph is a lie, as all photographs are. They're merely patterns of dots in varying shades of gray the eye perceives as an image, the way your mother weaves threads around pins but sees the whole as a pattern of lace, which in truth is only air enclosed by thread. Yes, every picture is a lie. Left is right and right is left. The brain fools itself into believing the fiction of the photograph.

Consider this other photograph, the one of Lelio and me. Brothers, partners, friends? In the studio, he pranced around like the *prima donna* that he is, grabbed me around the neck, and kissed the side of my head. I punched him lightly in the gut, and he bent over as if I'd really hurt him.

"Who do you think you are, baby brother?" he taunted me as he always does. "A regular Jack Dempsey?" He clocked me hard under the chin.

I take my sharpest tailoring scissors and cut along my image in the photograph with Lelio, follow the crisp outlines of my suit along my brother's shoulder, slice right through his neck to the other side. With embroidery scissors, I trim away my wrist and hand next to Lelio's head, consider the fragments of his mutilated figure, and wonder if he suspects his wife, your Aunt Theresa, and me.

I paint rubber cement on the back of my two-dimensional head and body and the tiny shards of my ringless left hand, press these images into the space next to Annina and you, and arrange my disembodied hand on her shoulder. The doctored photograph fits neatly under the glass of a gold picture frame I've purchased especially for this purpose. For a long time, I polish the glass with a clean cloth. You're alive. You're dead. I love you. I can't love you. It's impossible, but it's so.

I sit on the front porch holding my framed photograph and watch the young boys play stickball in the street. One of them is named Luca. I imagine he's you, banging his stick on the sewer cap, shouting at Nico to put it right down the middle. Nico winds up like Lefty Grove, but he releases the ball too soon and it beans Luca on the temple. Luca throws his stick down and howls. Suddenly, there are mothers everywhere. Where did they come from? Luca's mother picks him up, examines his head, and sends him back into the game with a kiss and a pat on his backside.

Inside again, I place the photograph on the mantel next to that of a young man who was once carefree enough to pose with his brother and good friends playing *scopa* on a Saturday night. Now an aging man stares back at me from the shine of polished glass.

ADDRESS

30 September 1928   Philadelphia

Dear Antonio,

I understand why you feel you must leave
Italy. Yet I must beg you to stay with
Annina. If you leave her behind, I'm afraid
she may never join me here when the time
comes next year.

It's unfair of me to ask, I know. But I
assure you that it's an illusion to think you
can start life over. Dreams do not change,
not there, not here. They are only dreams.

Greetings, Vincent

S. Antonio Giove
Roccamaro, Italy

BLACK TUESDAY

I. DEPARTURE

True to his long-ago promise, Vincenzo wired me the money for a first-class ticket from Naples to New York. And not just for any ship, but one of the newest, most beautifully appointed ships sailing that route, the MS *Vulcania*. Such extravagance! But when I got to thinking of hobnobbing with women dripping with furs and diamonds and men dressed in fancy top hats and tails, not to mention the cost, I thought to settle for second class.

"Nonsense," Papà said. "You've waited seven years for this voyage. And besides, how many times are you going to cross the Atlantic?"

I swallowed hard because his words reminded me that once in America, I might never see him or Antonio again. My brother was supposed to come with me, but Mamma insisted that he stay behind. "Who else will watch over me in my old age but my good son?" was how she put it. Perhaps for once, Mamma was right. I'll have Vincenzo and his brother Lelio and his sister-in-law, Theresa, and she'll have Papà and her son. Poor Antonio. His heart had been set for so long on America.

I fretted about how I'd fool those upper-class passengers into believing I was one of them. The English Sister Benedict had taught me in my primary school years was rusty, though the nun spent hours and hours before my departure helping me brush up on the language. She assured me that many of the first-class passengers would have thick accents, if they spoke

English at all.

Then there were my clothes. "You've been wearing black for far too long," Papà said. "It doesn't suit you."

Of course, he was right. Two years of black dresses, black veils, black gloves. Suits of armor meant to last only a year. Maybe if I dwelled on joy...but lately joy seemed to me a happy accident. The four years my precious Luca was on this earth, I experienced so much joy that I was fooled into thinking it would go on forever.

In the days leading up to my departure, Papà sewed feverishly night and day making outfits for me from the finest materials: a red silk dress with pearl buttons down the back; a navy serge suit composed of a calf-length skirt and a jacket fastened with ornate brass buttons; a black dress in the new "flapper" style with tiers of fringe that swayed as I walked; and my wedding dress refashioned into a stunning, cream-colored ball gown with an empire waist and a princess neckline. While Papà worked, I busied myself making accessories—a fascinator crowned with white lace and feathers, wool berets in a variety of colors, and two pairs of velvety kid gloves. I purchased three pairs of fine silk stockings, seamed down the back, the type I'd never before allowed myself the luxury. My cousin Mano—Roccamaro's only cobbler, but a superb one—made two pairs of shoes and one pair of boots designed to go with the new outfits.

Just days before I was to leave, I stood on a platform in my parents' bedroom in front of the only full-length mirror in the house and admired the gown. Papà knelt behind me with pins in his mouth making last-minute nips and tucks. Mamma came into the room and looked at my reflection in the mirror.

"Almost perfect," she said. She shooed Papà out of the way and lifted something over my head. I saw that it was her most treasured possession—a three-stranded necklace made of graduated pearls, Papà's wedding gift to her.

I ran my fingers along the beads, dumbstruck. After all we'd been through, after all the recriminations and silent tears. "I can't," I finally managed to say.

"Of course you can," she said.

I noticed that Papà had tears in his eyes, but I pretended not to see.

Finally, it was time for packing. Antonio gave me the steamer trunk he'd used when he shipped out for the war, the one he would have used had he been able to accompany me. It was made of deep brown leather, marred only by a few odd scuffs. Someone in his company had sent it back to us after he was hospitalized to recover from the burns and gas attack he suffered during the Great War. I remember when the trunk arrived with his belongings inside how Mamma howled at the sight, thinking it was confirmation of his death. But he'd lived. Now I was to leave him behind, fragile as he still was.

He and I filled the trunk together. At the bottom I placed my lace-making tools—the bobbins and pins, the cylindrical pillow, and my favorite patterns. My wardrobe came next. Antonio folded and refolded the garments, wrapping each separately in tissue paper and arranging the items so that not one square centimeter of space was wasted. The very last item was the white nightgown and peignoir I'd used on my wedding night and hadn't worn since. I blushed as he folded the layers of silk, both embarrassed by my brother touching such private things and by imagining myself with Vincenzo again as if for the first time. Although we'd been husband and wife for many years, we'd be strangers in bed. The seven years that had passed since we'd last been intimate seemed like a wholly different life.

Antonio smoothed more tissue across the top of the clothing and looked up at me. He grasped my chin in his hands and, as if reading my mind, pulled from his pocket one of Luca's wooden trucks, toys I thought I'd buried with him. I gasped, then burst into tears.

"Everything that is meant to be," he said, spinning the truck's front wheels and tucking it carefully between layers of clothing.

Just as when Antonio drove Vincenzo and me to Naples

seven years before to see my husband off to the new world, he insisted on driving me to the dock. This time, Mamma and Papà came with us, bouncing along in the back seat of the same truck we'd borrowed years ago. Mamma insisted we all dress in our best clothes for the journey, despite the chance of them becoming soiled from the dust kicked up from the often-rudimentary roads. I chose my new blue serge suit, for October had already grown quite chilly.

As we drove along, I couldn't help but think what a difference seven years made.

Back then I was a young woman, newly pregnant with Luca, fighting nausea the whole way. Now I was thirty-seven, Luca dead, me possibly past time to have another child. Let alone the terrifying thought of bringing another son or a daughter into the world. Then, as now, we weren't impoverished. We had the money to send Vincenzo second class, and we did so to avoid the anxiety and humiliations of Ellis Island, stories we'd heard about from those who traveled third class or steerage. All of Vincenzo's worldly belongings fit into a small trunk held together with leather straps. Now I had a first-class ticket and a wardrobe of brand-new clothes, a box of costumes to try on night after night on the eleven-day crossing.

One thing was exactly as before on that long-ago drive— Antonio's incessant tapping on the steering wheel. Knowing it was impossible to quiet his hands, I spent the ride distracting myself by watching the Italian countryside slide past my window, memorizing every windrow, every stalwart cypress, the hills where sheep grazed oblivious to my tears.

At the dock, Mamma once again became *la dolentissima madre*. She thumped one fist against her heart, shedding tears such as those at Ernestina's and Luca's funerals.

"I'm not dead," I said, but we both knew we'd never see each other again. I should have been kind. My only excuse was that the trip had exhausted me, and I was anxious about what lay ahead.

She inhaled deeply, trying to staunch her tears. Papà

handed her a white handkerchief, which she used to dab her eyes and loudly blow her nose. I would have been embarrassed at her ostentatious display except that everyone around us seemed similarly distraught.

An officious-looking man stopped in front of us and asked for my traveling papers—ticket, passport, and health certificate. He spent what seemed like an inordinate amount of time comparing my face to the passport photograph. Did I imagine the raised eyebrow when he looked at the first-class ticket and then at each of us in turn?

"Everything seems to be in order," he said, and handed the papers back. A steward followed close behind, helpfully informing me how to find my berth. He heaved my trunk on his shoulder and carried it up the gangplank.

It was time for good-byes. I hugged Mamma, gave her a peck on each cheek, and turned to my father. "Papà," I said. "Papà…"

He put a finger to my lips, placed his hands on my shoulders, and looked at me as if he were memorizing my face. Finally, he hugged me and kissed me on both cheeks and retreated to Mamma, wrapping his arm around her.

Last was Antonio's turn to say good-bye. He pulled me to him and almost wrung the breath out of me. He was shaking. "Oh, Antonio," I said. "Everything that is meant to be." That calmed him. Then I whispered in his ear, "Someday you'll join me. Mamma can't live forever."

It was a terrible thing to say, but we both started laughing.

He kissed me on both cheeks, stepped back, and put his arm around Papà. I walked to the gangplank and up its steep incline, turning and waving every few steps. On deck, I pushed my way to secure a place along the railing. There, I blew kisses and waved my own white lace handkerchief, mirroring Mamma, until she turned away. Afterward I just stood, holding onto the railing as if my life depended on it, until the foghorn sounded, and the ship made its slow way from the dock.

II. *ISOLA DELLA SPERANZA, ISOLA DELLE LACRIME*

I've started smoking again, a filthy habit. I crush an empty pack of unfiltered Camels, throw it in a nearby trash can, and open a new pack, my third of the day. What would Annina think? I fretted over my weakness, but waiting on the dock, impatient for the arrival of the *Vulcania*, I had no choice.

I'd never been to Manhattan before. Or more precisely, I'd only set foot on this dock for the time it took me to walk from the *Providence* to the barge that transported me to Ellis Island. I'd told Annina I was sailing second class, but in truth I'd traveled steerage. What was the harm in a little lie?

I remember my arrival well. First- and second-class passengers were allowed to disembark in Manhattan. I envied them being greeted by friends and relatives while I crowded onto a barge full of third-class and steerage passengers. I remember the shadow of Lady Liberty falling across the barge. My anxiety was quelled somewhat by her majestic presence, her torch held high, and the promise that my fellow immigrants had written to me—*Give me your tired, your poor, your huddled masses yearning to breathe free.* I couldn't imagine such a generous country would turn me away. Was this to be my island of hope or my island of tears?

I'd managed to avoid the illnesses that swept through steerage, but it was impossible to avoid the communal stench that arose from our unwashed bodies. With the ship's manifest number pinned to my jacket, I joined what seemed to be an impossibly long queue that wound up an enormous flight of stairs to a great hall and into a registry room and yet another long line controlled by metal railings. There, we were given medical exams. It didn't matter that I had a certificate of disinfection and vaccination issued at the port of Naples. Who could blame the Americans? Any number of diseases might have been picked up during the voyage.

I watched as some immigrants were marked with chalk and sent to the island's hospital. Those white slashes haunt me to this day. When my turn finally came, the doctor poked and prodded, flashed a light in my eyes, and made me stick out my tongue.

"Go," he said.

Relief. Two minutes, after waiting hours.

He pointed to another queue snaking slowly to the immigration inspectors, who would interrogate us with the twenty-nine questions Lelio had sent to me ahead of time. Before I left, I spent long hours with Father Gaetano—the very same priest who had taught me English in school—memorizing twenty-nine answers in perfect English. The key, my brother had written, was to assure the inspector that you had a trade, foreign currency worth $50, and a job waiting. I must credit Lelio this: he'd paved the way two years before by establishing a successful tailoring business.

When it was my turn, the inspector asked for my name and then ran his finger down to *Desiderio, Vincenzo* on the "manifest of alien passengers." I suppose the Americans thought we'd arrived from another world. He read aloud across a line of neatly typewritten information, checking the boxes as he went. Age, nationality, height, eye and hair color, and so forth.

"It says here *peasant* under occupation," he said, pointing to the box. "Do you have a means of gainful employment?"

"I'm a *tailor*," I replied. "My brother has a job for me in Philadelphia."

In the old world, tailors were thought of as artisans, but I have since discovered that here in America, we're considered manual laborers. Perhaps that's why the inspector wrinkled his nose when I said I was a tailor, though it was certainly a step up from peasant. He scribbled *taylor* in the box and continued with the interrogation. I must admit that his misspelling gave me a certain satisfaction.

When the interview was over, he directed me to another set of stairs, called the Stairs of Separation. Those who passed the exams went down one side and those who failed down the other. A free man at last aboard the ferry to New Jersey, I breathed in American air. I remember the taste of that air, like the coolest, freshest spring water. Lady Liberty lay behind me and Lelio ahead on the Hoboken dock.

III. CROSSING TO AMERICA

First class was so much more than I expected. My stateroom was small but elegantly appointed. I'd paid for a room without a balcony (certain luxuries seemed a touch too wasteful), but I did have a porthole that looked out onto the sea. The bed was enclosed with satin drapes adorned with white and green leaves on a cream-colored background. There was a mahogany dresser with more drawers than my clothes could fill. A vase with pink roses secured a card with my dinner table assignment.

That first night on board, I wore my red silk dress and Mamma's pearl necklace, carefully straightened the seams of my stockings, and fixed my hair in a loose bun. The dining room was a marvel: two stories high, each table set with fine linens and sterling silver and flanked by purple velvet chairs. Palm trees lined the walls between windows that framed the sea. Above, an ornately carved ceiling held enormous iron chandeliers.

I found my table and sat down, anxious to see who my dining companions would be. I supposed they'd seat me with three of the snobbish ladies, who, like me, were traveling without their husbands. Imagine my surprise when a young American couple with a seven-year-old son greeted me.

"Hiya," the boy said. "My name is Michael Robinson. This is my second trip across the ocean. Well, I guess it's my first trip going this way. I live in New York. What do you think they'll have for dinner? I'm starving."

"Michael, dear, give the nice lady a chance to introduce herself," his mother said. She turned to me, blushing. "He's a bit overexcited, I think. I'm Anne and this is my husband, John."

I smiled. "I'm Anne, too. Well, Anna, actually," I said.

"If you must know, my full name is Anna Maria Concetta Romano Robinson."

"And mine is Anna Maria Esther Giove Desiderio."

"My middle name is Romano," the boy piped up. "After my mom."

We all laughed. The names broke the ice. She was happy to carry on the conversation in Italian, which she claimed was rusty, and I was happy to practice my English.

In this way, the worst of my fears went unrealized.

The first-class women sitting on their deck chairs as I passed reminded me of Roccamaro's gossips who sat every day on the stone bench in front of San Ponziano. The arrogant women hid their faces behind elaborate fans while they whispered whatever they whispered. I surprised myself, held my head high as I passed, and fanned a Venetian fan far more beautiful than any of theirs. Sometimes I'd say something in carefully unaccented phrases I'd practiced over and over. "Good afternoon, ladies" or "What a pleasant day!" They seemed bewildered.

I much preferred the solitary time I spent in the reading room with its vaulted ceiling and carved wooden cabinets lined with thick leather books. Each day I chose a book at random—almost all of them in English—and whispered the words to myself. Very few people availed themselves of the room—they preferred to sit on the deck and watch the sea pass by—so I was free to practice my English both there and in the dining room as we sailed closer and closer to my rendezvous with Vincenzo.

Every evening we gathered on the deck to watch the "fireworks." First-class passengers mingled with everyone else, jostling to gain the best vantage point from which to view the nightly spectacle. They weren't real fireworks, of course. One of the stewards explained the phenomenon. To keep the funnel clean, the engineers put sand into the exhaust. The hot sand would rise up the funnel and scour the insides. When the white-hot sprays of sand flew into the sky, they lit up a bit like fireworks.

On our last evening together, the Robinsons and I shared two bottles of wine. Up till that night, I'd told them only the most pleasant things about my background—that I was meeting my husband, that my family lived in the city of Pescara (only a little bit of a lie), and so forth. That night, Michael had fallen asleep at the table, and, with my tongue loosened by alcohol, I mentioned that Vincenzo and I had been separated for seven years.

"How on earth?" Anne said.

"Politics," I replied.

"I don't know that I could be separated from my John for more than a week or two."

"The years seem to have flown by," I lied. "And besides, I had a brother to take care of. Antonio never got over fighting in the war."

There was a pause and then John said, "My oldest brother... died at Belleau Wood."

"I'm so sorry," I said. "That war. Let's hope it really was the war to end all wars."

A steward came by to hand out a sheet containing the news of the day—October 28, 1929. I hadn't been paying attention, preferring to wait until our arrival to catch up on current events. Anne and I continued chatting while John looked over the broadsheet.

"Anything wrong?" Anne asked.

He patted her hand. "No, no," he said. "Just some trouble in the stock market."

He folded the sheet in quarters and put it in his pocket.

At that moment, the band started playing, a signal for those who wished to dance to make their way to the dance floor. The music woke up Michael. We watched his parents dance a slow waltz and then a brisk Charleston. They came back to the table, laughing and sweating.

"Would you like to dance?" John asked.

"I'm afraid my card is full," I said. "But you two look great out there. Why don't I take Michael back to my room while you enjoy yourselves a little longer?"

"Well, it's past his bedtime," Anne said.

"I'm not sleepy," Michael said, crossing his arms in a gesture that reminded me of Luca when he was overtired.

"Are you sure it's not an imposition?" John asked.

"Not at all." I offered my hand to Michael.

In my stateroom, I pulled out the wooden truck Antonio had so carefully secreted among my treasures. Michael and I spent the better part of an hour making roads with tissue paper and running the truck along the floor. When his parents came to retrieve him, he offered the truck to me. Before his parents could object, I said, "You keep it as a memento. I won't be needing it."

IV. AT THE DOCK

This past year, I renounced my allegiance to Victor Emmanuel III and became an American citizen. Never again would I have to go through the humiliations of Ellis Island if I ever traveled back to Italy. I couldn't bear the thought of Annina going through the same indignities no matter what it cost me. She'd find out soon enough that it was more than an extravagance to have her travel first class. But how could I have foreseen that the roaring twenties would come crashing to a halt on the very day of her arrival, October 29, 1929? Who would believe such bad timing? Yes, what were the chances that between the day of her departure on October 18 and the day of her arrival, the American economy would collapse?

Another coincidence: I waited for her on the very dock I'd crossed only in passing seven years ago on my way to Ellis Island. Cigarette after cigarette burned down to ash. I crushed each one out on those wooden boards with my shoe.

A newsboy wove through the crowd selling the latest *New York Times* blaring the headline STOCK PRICES SLUMP $14,000,000,000 IN NATIONWIDE STAMPEDE TO UNLOAD. Fourteen billion! The number was mind-boggling. And this news followed on the heels of a week of panic selling. I gave him two cents for a copy. Fortunately, I had no money invested in the market, but I knew that such events would touch every American. I'd always kept part of my money in a small safe in my home, and I'd withdrawn about half of my savings from the bank at the first signs of trouble this past summer. Now my bank had closed its doors, temporarily they said. I comforted myself with the knowledge that I had a steady job. People needed clothes, no matter what happened.

I'd come to Manhattan in my Model T. One last extravagance. One of my wealthier clients had offered to buy it for a decent price, considering the circumstances. I asked him if the sale could wait until after I picked up my wife. I wanted to escort Annina back to Philadelphia in style. What is it the Bible tells us? *Pride goeth before destruction, and a haughty spirit before a fall.* Guilty as charged.

V. ARRIVAL

The *Vulcania* slid along a long gray pier in New York Harbor. The first thing I noticed as we docked was a castle on a far hill, across the bay. *Imagine,* I thought, *to live in such a place. America is a fairy tale. Perhaps Vincenzo and I are a prince and princess, and it's time to live happily ever after.*

I made my way along the railing to the front of the ship and tried to spot Vincenzo in the crowd lining the dock. No one looked familiar. Was it possible he'd forgotten the date of my arrival? If so, what would I do once I'd gotten through customs? I comforted myself knowing that I could exchange my lire for fifty dollars and that I had his home address in my purse. If worse came to worst. Surely there were buses or trains to Philadelphia.

As I stood in the first-class line in the customs house, my throat felt dry. I concentrated on suppressing the cough that was rising in my throat. I distracted myself from the tickle by practicing English in my head, anticipating the questions the agent might ask.

When my turn came, I handed my papers to the inspector.

He looked them over, quickly checking off boxes on the ship's manifest and scribbling words I couldn't make out upside down. "Is someone waiting for you here?" he asked.

"My husband," I said. Two simple words, the only English I needed.

He handed back my papers and said, "Welcome to America."

As I made my way outside to the waiting crowd, who would be in front of me but Michael and his parents? Michael held the wooden truck I'd given him. He turned to me and smiled. "Good-bye, Miss Anna," he said, then ran ahead of his parents and jumped into the waiting arms of an elderly couple, who buried him in kisses.

At the edge of the crowd, I searched for Vincenzo. My heart raced. I felt like I couldn't breathe. Then, as if in a fairy tale, the crowd parted and there he was!

His hair had gone completely gray. His face was lined, his teeth and the fringe of his hair were yellowed by tobacco. As ridiculous as it sounds, my first thought was to break him of his smoking habit. Seven years, and this was my first thought. My next thought was to find comfort in his aging as I, too, had aged. Yes, there was a flash that felt like satisfaction. Small comfort in that. Small comforts, like beads on a rosary or the fine knots in an intricate bobbin lace. So what if he wasn't the prince I'd imagined once upon a time?

His blue eyes were veiled, impossible to read. He'd seen oceans in them. Vast continents had swallowed him up and given him back to me. He took a single step toward me.

"Is that you, Annina?"

So he *had* forgotten me. Now he would remember.

He gathered me in his arms, and I fell into him.

A steward appeared out of nowhere, the very same steward who'd attended me throughout the crossing, and placed my trunk at our feet. Everything I owned was in that trunk, everything I cherished left behind—Papà and Antonio, and Luca, his bones a pattern under earth. Might I have carried my son with me to America, what was left of him in the purse dangling from my wrist, the three of us together at last?

PART III: EVERYTHING THAT IS MEANT TO BE

THE WHITE NIGHTGOWN

I grew up with the white nightgown. It hung on a dressmaker's dummy in the corner of my bedroom. My mother, Anna, had draped it there, carefully, as if the dummy were human and not just a life-sized doll. The nightgown was made of fine silk, smooth as glass turned almost to liquid. I loved running my hands over it. The gown was sleeveless, with a plunging neckline and an empire waist from which flowed yards and yards of pure white fabric. The hem was edged with an intricately patterned lace that Mom called eyelash chantilly. She'd made the gown for her trousseau, she once told me, during the time she waited for her husband to return from a World War I Austrian prison camp to their home in Italy. As I grew older, I wondered about the timing—why did Mom make her wedding night costume *after* she was wed? I hesitated to ask. The question seemed too private, along with a host of other questions it might raise.

As a little girl, I thought of the nightgown as a plaything. Sometimes I'd take it down and try it on. Of course, it puddled like a white lake all around me. Once, my mother caught me playing dress up, but instead of chastising me, she merely smiled and said, "Rosemarie, you look so grown up."

Mom was a wartime bride. In 1915, my father, Vincenzo (who became Vincent in America), enlisted with his three brothers immediately after Italy entered the war on the Allies' side. At the time, he believed in the Italian cause to reclaim parts of the Austro-Hungarian empire for his homeland. Only after Pop returned in 1919 from his time as a POW did he realize that the

Italians had *made a deal with the devil*, as he liked to say, and never regained all that they had been promised by the Allies.

Before he deployed, my parents married in a hasty civil ceremony. My maternal grandmother, whom I called Nonna though I never met her, insisted. She had her eye on my father's family home at the top of the hill in Roccamaro and gambled that by war's end, she might move up to that coveted house from their home at the bottom of the hill. Of course, her fondest wish depended on people dying—Pop's mother and father and two of their sons obliged. Uncle Lelio lived but emigrated to America soon after the war ended.

Pop hardly ever spoke of the war and his imprisonment. "Rosie," he'd say, "that was so long ago."

Mom would tell me he was fortunate because the camp's Commandant needed a tailor, and Pop was a master of that craft. *Fortunate.* Such an odd way to describe what befell him. Much later, I realized he had what they call survivor's guilt. In addition to two of his brothers, ten thousand Italians died at Caporetto alone.

My parents endured a second separation after Pop left for America in 1922. What was to be a year or two of separation became much longer when Mussolini decreed that wives had to stay behind for seven years before joining their husbands abroad. Il Duce wanted the money that would flow back to a war-decimated Italy from the prosperous émigrés. Or homesick men would return to Italy once and for all.

*　　*　　*

What does all this family history have to do with the white nightgown? It was only after I was engaged to Frank that I understood. Mom was dying, and she wanted to make sure I knew what was involved in marriage. Sex, that is. We'd never spoken about it, but of course by then—I was twenty-two—I understood the basics even though I was a virgin.

Confined to bed by the infirmities of heart failure, Mom could hardly walk as she struggled to breathe. One day near the end of her life, the Saturday after Thanksgiving in 1953, I'd helped her bathe and change into fresh nightclothes. As I balled her soiled garments into the hamper by her bed, she touched my arm.

"Let me get these in the wash first," I said.

"The laundry can wait," she said, gently squeezing my arm. "I want you to have something for your trousseau. There, in the cedar chest."

I opened the chest at the foot of her bed, which was filled with the lace and linens she'd made during her lifetime. I'd always loved a throw she'd crocheted in an intricate pattern of overlapping diamonds. The throw lay on top, and I lifted it into the air.

"This?" I asked.

"Of course you can have that. But farther down is a peignoir. It matches the nightgown hanging in your bedroom. Can you get them?"

I returned with the nightgown, dug out the peignoir from the chest, and laid both across her lap.

"I've told you that Pop and I married in a civil ceremony just before he shipped out. What I didn't tell you is that your *nonna* forbade us from...being together...because the Church hadn't yet consecrated our marriage."

I understood what "being together" meant. Even on her deathbed, she struggled to put into words what she felt I needed to know.

"It was only after the war and our church wedding that Pop and I shared the same bed."

So that's why she made the peignoir set *after* they were first married. The delay also helped explain why it took so long for them to have a baby. But even after their church wedding, it took four years.

"In my heart, I felt that by making fine things such as this for the future, there would be a future for us." She ran her hand over the nightgown and sighed. "Pop suffered terribly in those first months back from the war. Every night, I put on this nightgown, and every night I held him, hoping. And finally, my patience was rewarded."

She paused to catch her breath, a reflex that had become an effort of late. "I thought it was a simple thing to have a baby. But getting pregnant took two more years. And in the sort of bad luck that stalked our family, I had a miscarriage. Then I got pregnant with your brother Luca just before your father left for America. I kept it a secret because I didn't want to alter our plans. What was the harm in waiting? We'd be reunited soon enough, I thought, then the three of us could start over in America. A few months after Pop left came Mussolini's unexpected declaration."

She began to cough, a continuous wheezing that erupted from deep inside her lungs. I poured a glass of water from a carafe on her bedside table, sat down beside her on the bed, and waited for the episode to pass.

She took a sip and swallowed, then rested her head against my shoulder. "Those first few years in Italy weren't unhappy, Rosie dear. I'd hate to leave you with that impression. I had Papà and Antonio. You couldn't ask for a more loving father or brother. My mother got her wish to move up the hill to Vincenzo's house. Side by side, my father and I worked together under the canopy of bougainvillea in front of Vincenzo's home. We were quite a team. Then Luca was born. I thought my life was almost complete."

She fingered the lace, tracing the delicate scallops along the hem. "I was making a bridal veil when the worst thing ever to happen to me...happened. Nonna and Luca were at the lake, enjoying a holiday picnic with friends and family."

She stopped again, wheezing, struggling to catch her breath. Water lapped over the edge of the glass she was holding. I took it from her and placed it on the nightstand.

"We can talk about this later," I said. She'd told me the story of Luca's death many times. My brother was a ghost, ever present, hovering over us. As sorry as I sometimes felt for myself trying to fill the hole his death left, I felt sorrier for my brother

Vinnie, who as their only living son had bigger shoes to fill.

And to think Pop never saw his firstborn son. I tried to imagine what it must have been like for him to receive such news—Luca dead from typhoid brought on by drinking water from the lake. After his death, and while my parents were still apart, Pop had inserted a cutout of himself into a photo of Mom and Luca. So carefully did he compose the doctored photo that for years I'd assumed the three of them had been together—ever so briefly—as a family. You had to look very closely to see the deception.

Recovered from her coughing fit, Mom raised the nightgown to me. "Here, try it on."

"No, no," I said. "I couldn't."

"Please," she said.

It seemed an odd request for a mother to see her daughter as she'd been seen by her husband on her long-ago wedding night. Until she became too ill to care for herself, I'd never even seen my mother stripped to her underwear, let alone naked, nor she me since I was a child. But what harm to indulge her?

Out of modesty, I suppose, she closed her eyes while I took off my pants and shirt and pulled on the nightgown and peignoir. I looked at myself in the full-length mirror that graced her armoire. The nightgown fit perfectly, the only hint of scandal the revealing neckline. The silk was exquisite but quite opaque, not like the sheer peignoir sets I'd been browsing in the Montgomery Ward catalogue and dreamed of wearing myself.

"You can open your eyes," I said, and she did.

She put her hand to her mouth and breathed a ragged breath. "Lovely," she said. "What do you think?"

"It *is* lovely," I said, because it *was* beautiful.

She patted the bed for me to sit beside her again, put her arm around me, and pulled me close. She smelled of lavender, the bath soap I'd just used to bathe her.

"The very day I arrived in America, the stock market crashed. Pop likes to say it was all my fault. America was brought to its knees by my beauty."

We laughed. "And Pop and you had to move in with Uncle Lelio and Aunt Theresa to pool your resources, etcetera, etcetera."

"Aunt Theresa," she said, shaking her head. "There are things you don't know."

She lay back and closed her eyes. I thought she'd fallen asleep, but no. "Your father and Theresa had an affair, you know, right under Lelio's nose. Imagine the two of them, carrying on while I was in Italy."

And just that suddenly, other pieces of our family history fell into place. Theresa had died of cancer four years before, and Mom had refused to go to her funeral. It caused a minor scandal in the neighborhood. Pop made excuses for her—Vinnie had some make-believe, unbreakable appointment. I thought the whole thing strange, Pop lying to cover for Mom. I knew there was bad blood between my mother and Aunt Theresa—you could feel the chill when the two were together—but I'd always assumed it was a petty misunderstanding. There were plenty of those in our extended family—Cousin Fiorella, who broke Mom's treasured soup tureen because she claimed it had been part of *her* family's heirloom china. Or Aunt Maria, who blamed my father for her family's penury during the Great Depression because he and Uncle Lelio wouldn't employ her *no-good son* in their tailor shop. Never mind that they had just enough work during that time to keep the two of them in business. Even Main Line ladies had limits to their fortunes during the Great Depression.

Twenty-five years had passed. What was the point of holding grudges? I loved my father. I sympathized with a man in the prime of his life who had been deprived of female companionship for seven years. I loved my mother, too, and understood that there were some transgressions that could never be forgiven.

Mom opened her eyes. "You don't seem surprised."

"It explains the funeral," I said. "Did Uncle Lelio know?"

"If he did, he never said."

I fingered the lace edging of the peignoir coat. "Tell me again how this is made."

And she did, something about bobbins and pins, the lace-making art I could never quite follow. She ran her hand over the silk fabric, still impossibly white, and traced the pattern of the lace she'd made so many years ago. As she talked, I imagined her in this very nightgown, probably feeling as anxious then as I did now about my forthcoming wedding night. Within months after she'd arrived in America, she was pregnant with me—at thirty-eight—and scared. She knew what it was to lose a child. Imagine that courage. Or faith.

*　　*　　*

My mother's Catholic faith seemed unshakeable, despite God dispensing so much suffering upon our family. I'd had my doubts. When I was ten, I smashed our best crucifix, one with a gold-plated Jesus nailed to a cross that hung over my parents' bed, the wood darkened with layers of stain and lacquer. It was Ash Wednesday. Mom chased me all over the house, insisting I accompany her to church to have my forehead blackened with ashes. To underscore my refusal, I jumped up on her bed, wrenched the cross from the wall, and brought it down on the iron bedframe.

I can see myself raising the broken fragment of the cross in my hand, triumphant in my renunciation of the drone of Sunday homilies, Tuesday novenas, and Saturday afternoon confessions. *What was so great about heaven?* I used to wonder. *The dead waiting for those they'd left behind? Luca, the brother I never knew, who was nevertheless everywhere?* I tried not to think about the time when he and I would finally meet. Anticipation was just more suffering. The moment these thoughts crossed my mind, I'd tuck them deep inside. Afraid of the all-seeing, all-knowing God, I went to bed every night praying He had more important things to worry about than an unrepentant child, even if she had reached "the age of reason." Still, I spent sleepless nights waiting to be found out, waiting for my own portion of punishment for the near occasion of sin.

* * *

My mother died ten days after Thanksgiving, on December 7, 1953. She was only sixty-one. In the hospital that day, I held her hand.

"How much longer?" she asked, gasping for breath even with the machine pumping oxygen into her fluid-filled lungs.

I begged the doctor to give her something to make her sleep, and he did. Such a relief after she'd spent days struggling just to breathe.

Odd thoughts persecuted me during my vigil. That day of ashes haunted me. As I waved the broken piece of wood high in the air, I saw Mom coming toward me, her face red, her hand raised. Fear replaced bravado. I ducked under her hand, hopped off the bed, and ran down the staircase of our row home and out the front door. The forward motion of my panic carried me off the curb and into the path of a Bond Bread truck out making deliveries. The tire left a permanent scar across my forehead. Mom counted it a miracle I lived, an answer to her prayers.

To ease my mind and comfort her, I recited the Rosary aloud using my fingers as phantom beads. It was a Monday, a day for the Joyful Mysteries. The fifth and final mystery seemed apt. Jesus had gone to Jerusalem with His parents for Passover, and upon their return, Joseph and Mary set out for Nazareth not realizing they'd left Jesus behind. They retraced their steps, full of grief and anxiety that they'd lost their Son, only to discover Him teaching in the Temple.

Mary asked, "Why have You done this to us? Your father and I have been searching for You in sorrow."

Jesus replied, "Don't be afraid. It's God's will be done."

As children we were taught that the meaning of this mystery lay in Mary's perseverance in the face of suffering. A mother keeps all things in her heart.

I said the Glory Be, world without end, and made the sign of the cross, first over myself and then over Mom. She was resting quietly, the oxygen machine humming in the corner of the hospital room. What came to me as I watched over her was the definition of grace we'd memorized from the *Baltimore Catechism* in preparation for First Holy Communion. *Grace,* it says, *is the supernatural help of God, which enlightens our mind and strengthens our will to do good and to avoid evil.* Hail Anna, full of grace.

On her death certificate, verified with a doctor's illegible signature, is the "disease or condition directly leading to death": *Acute myocardial infarct.* Scrawled underneath, in the space for "antecedent causes": *Congestive heart failure.* Her heart had finally given out.

*　　*　　*

I had no intention of wearing her white nightgown on my wedding night. Instead, I'd splurged on a nylon set from the Montgomery Ward catalogue for $14.94 from the salary I earned as a secretary. A small fortune, nearly half my weekly wage. The sheer peignoir set promised to make me "a vision of beauty, with lavish lace spilling down the front of the coat, around the cuffs of the sleeves, and along the hem of the bare gown." I imagined this was what an American girl wore on her wedding night. Nylon, not silk. A modern invention.

As soon as the package arrived, I ran upstairs to try it on. I shimmied into the nightgown and then the coat, which fastened with a single, oversized button. Staring at myself in my full-length mirror, my body clearly visible underneath, I swayed this way and that, trying to imagine Frank's reaction to such a flimsy piece of clothing. Though it looked quite lovely, I had to admit that the fabric was a pale imitation of silk, and that the lace lacked the delicate quality of my mother's handiwork.

Her nightgown stood on the dressmaker's dummy in the corner of my bedroom all through my last days as a secretary, my nights in my parents' bedroom holding my mother's hand, and finally those last precious days at Mercy Fitzgerald Hospital.

The Christmas season was upon us, and against her wishes, we spent the holidays mourning her passing. She'd insisted I go ahead with our wedding plans for the coming May even though she knew she wouldn't live to see me walk down the aisle.

"I'll have none of this mourning for what can't be," she said.

On my wedding day, the sun shone brightly, purple lilacs bloomed profusely in the narrow garden along the side of the church. The May Procession had just been held. Children had crowned an alabaster statue of Mary with a wreath of lilies and laid roses at her feet. Pop walked me down the aisle, Vinnie Junior served as best man, my cousins and friends rounded out the wedding party. In the photos from that day, everyone is smiling, even Pop.

Frank and I spent our wedding night at the Bellevue Stratford in downtown Philly. Packed in my suitcase was my mother's peignoir set. Behind the closed door of the hotel bathroom, I put on the white nightgown. The silk slid down my body, the lace whispered against my neck. I called through the door to ask Frank to turn off the lights. Then I opened the door and stood silhouetted against its frame. In the pale dark, I could see Frank smiling at me. I smiled back. A miracle, this happiness.

THE RED BERET

When I was a little girl, I played at my father's feet, watched his sewing machine's angry treadle whir like the pistons of a freight train, his head bent to the plunging needle, his lips sucking straight pins and unfiltered Camel cigarettes. Only when I entered fifth grade did I realize his thimble finger was yellow, he laughed in all the wrong places, told stories of the old world in heavily accented English, as if my friends cared where he came from, as if they understood.

Every year without fail, he sewed me a beautiful wool coat and a red beret. I was one of the few children who sported a new ensemble each winter, the privilege of being a tailor's daughter. And yet. I threw those berets in the garbage can in the alley behind our Philadelphia row home, where the fruit-and-vegetable man flirted with our mothers at the back door, sold "Tomaaatoooes, 10 for a dolla, apples, 50 cents a dozen, water-rr-melon, fresh and cold." Dyed the color of a clown's nose, those berets pierced my head like a crown of thorns, separated me from the blue-eyed, straight-haired American girls.

In high school, I never invited Pop to the annual father-daughter dances. I threw those invitations in the garbage too.

When I became a mother, he became my child. Paralyzed by strokes, he splashed in the sunlight in a wheelchair by the living room window, blanket to chin. It no longer mattered that he spoke accented English since he could no longer speak.

Like Mom, his heart was the problem. Aortic stenosis, the doctors told me. They decided to try something experimental—

to replace the narrowing valve with an artificial one. They cut his chest open, then sewed it shut. His heart was enlarged, his lungs too black, they said. There was nothing they could do.

94

SIGN LANGUAGE

Vincent wakes to the tug of tape being ripped from his right eye—his daughter Rose's "good morning," this sudden, almost pleasurable sting. Sunlight floods his permanently open right eye. She doesn't think he feels pain there, so she isn't gentle. She's half-right. Physical pain isn't what he feels, not on his right side. The sensation is more like coming to consciousness after a bad dream—the comfort of the familiar bed, its sharp angles and flat soft surface somehow distorted. On the edge, falling, catching his fall. The bed firmly under him. Everything is exactly as he left it the night before: his memory fraying, Rose fussing, his wife, Annina, gone.

Every morning, this tearing away. Rose peels him, layer by layer. *A fruit*, he thinks, *an overripe pear whose skin takes with it part of the pulp.* Thin parchment is all that's left between him and bones.

"Pop?" Rose says, her cheek hovering over his mouth, checking, no doubt, to make sure he's still breathing. He hasn't opened his good left eye, and the right one lolls in its socket. He holds his breath, ashamed but curious, wondering what she'll do.

"Pop?" she says again, more urgently. She slaps him lightly on the left cheek. "Pop?"

He's waiting for his Annina. Maybe she'll come to him as bones. Her cheekbone against his cheek. Her kiss, all incisors and jawbone. He's been waiting for flesh, but maybe all that's left is bone. He shudders, opens his left eye, and stares at his flesh-and-blood daughter. *Just a bad dream.*

"You scared me to death," she says.

Her face is so close that the heat of her breath warms his

cheek. There's a tear in her right eye, a single bead of water stuttering on the rim of her lower lid. So she'd cry, and then—what? The tears would dry.

She presses her hand against his chest, brushes her lips over his forehead. Her dark, curly hair falls over his face. *So much like my wife*, Vincent thinks, closing his eye again. Annina bends to kiss him, her fingers undoing his shirt buttons even as he fastens them. He pretends to be annoyed as he winds her long hair once, twice, three times around his hand, pulls her head back, and kisses her down the length of her throat. She's finally come back to him after so many years.

Something touches his shoulder. He opens his eye. No, only Rose, not his dead wife.

Rose pushes the rolling table on which she's placed a breakfast tray over his bed, fiddles with the toggles on the control panel, and adjusts his body until his position approximates sitting up. Straining the good muscles in his back, he manages to lift his head and smile lopsidedly.

Without returning the smile, she thrusts a spoon in his hand and asks, "What would you like for lunch today?"

Lunch? Not that he remembers each day's rhythm, but how has the morning already escaped him?

Steam curls from a bowl of hot baby cereal on the breakfast tray. *Thank the Lord, still morning.* He stirs slow figure eights through the mush while he considers her question, his response, her likely "no." He lets go of the spoon and drums his fingers on his thigh, his signal for the alphabet board he uses to communicate with her. Since his second stroke, he can't speak, so that although he thinks he's said the word for *broken* or *no*, all that comes from his mouth is a long O. He can gesture—a nod for *yes*, a headshake for *no*, hand movements that mean *come* and *go* and *please*—but his left hand trembles so badly when he holds it up too long that sometimes it's hard for anyone to tell what he wants.

Rose retrieves the board from the clutter of framed photographs on the nightstand that she's placed there to remind him of his family. He flexes his good left hand (what he thinks of as his good hand, though this past week, the left has been troubling him as well) and points to the letter "F." He pauses, then finishes the word: "-AGIOLI." Even without looking, he senses her frown.

She folds her arms across her chest. "You know what happened the last time we tried that. If I hadn't heard the glass breaking..."

The words dangle between them like a dare. He knows she won't say, "You could have died." He knows she won't say, "I don't want you to die." Instead she says, "You've hardly touched your breakfast."

She heaps the spoon with cereal and holds it out to him. Taking the spoon from her hand, he tongues a tiny portion into his mouth, works it to the back of his throat, and swallows. If he concentrates, he might be able to eat enough to avoid another scene with his daughter. There have been too many of those lately. Last week it was a bowl of *pasta e fagioli*. Although she'd cut the pasta into miniature pieces, he'd managed to get a bean stuck in his windpipe. He gasped for breath—instinct over reason—and knocked over his water glass. She came running, knelt beside him on the bed, and slapped him hard on his back. The white bean flew out of his mouth and bounced off the bedpost. He replays the scene backward, the bean flying toward him, growing larger, lodging again in his windpipe. He doesn't flail this time, doesn't break the glass. Time continues reversing, leaping backward a dozen years. 1953. Annina's heart beating erratically in its cage until it stops altogether. 1932. Baby Vinnie sliding through the birth canal. 1931. Rose untaking her first step. Spooling. 1929. The dock in Manhattan, Annina walking unsteadily up the MS *Vulcania*'s gangplank, away from him, unwiping tears. 1922. His own boat, the *Providence*, sailing backward across the Atlantic to the Naples dock and he traveling up the Gran Sasso to his tailoring chair in the doorway of his home in Roccamaro. The spool rewinds steadily, searching for the crucial moment that brought him here, until all that's left is the flapping of grainy, translucent film, circling the reel, clicking endlessly in the whitewash of light, and the silhouette of grown-up Rose hovering at the edges of his vision.

The result of the *white-bean moment*, as he's come to think of it, is clear: she'll no longer leave him alone when he eats.

He forces another sip from the spoon. The faint taste of metal caused by one of the drugs he takes makes him want to gag.

"So what do you want for lunch?"

Vincent pulls the board toward him. "NOTHING," he spells.

"How about some of that nice pea soup we had for dinner the other night?"

He pretends to stick his finger down his throat.

"Knock it off. I'm in no mood to argue. The weather's too beautiful," she says, opening the window. "See?"

The sour odor Vincent imagines as that of his own body decaying is replaced by the scent of newly mown grass. Rose picks up the mug of black coffee from the breakfast tray, handle-side out, and holds it toward him. He grasps the cup and blows across the surface, waiting for his hand to stop shaking before he attempts a sip.

She stares at him. "Didn't you hear what I said?" she asks. "You haven't told me what you want for lunch."

He puts down the coffee mug and begins to spell again, "W" and "H" and "A" and "T." The tips of his fingers tremble. He reaches "I" and flexes his hand, then "WANT." The spasm in his hand, the same erratic tremor he'd experienced for several days before his second stroke, the one that kept him up last night, prevents him from continuing. His thumb jerks toward his middle finger arrhythmically, the fingers snapping out of sync.

She takes his hand in hers. "You know you only get these when you haven't done your exercises. You haven't been, have you." This isn't a question, so he doesn't have to lie about squeezing the stupid rubber ball. As she massages his hand, the ineffectual snapping subsides.

Placing his hand over the board, she says, "Tell me what

you want."

Vincent stretches his hand out like a starfish, thinking one simple word. *Annina.* He worries now that she won't come, just as he worried until he saw her on the New York dock that she wouldn't buy the ticket for which he'd saved seven years, that she'd stay in Italy with her parents and her brother, Antonio, cloistered in the doorway of their home that was once his home, weaving bridal lace, not living or dying, forever there, a ghost to him. But she came then; she'll come now. He points to "A," to "N" and "N," and stops.

"ANN?" she asks. But she moves her head back and forth, as if she knows what he wishes to spell.

He studies her face, then the board. The "N" seems to have swollen, its black bars bulging out toward the "M" and "O." His hand begins to shake again. He rubs it against his leg, replaces it on the board. He finds "T," spells rapidly "HINGS-I-CANT-HAV—"

His hand won't stop shaking. He bangs it against the board, and Rose pulls the table away. He continues punching, the blows falling on his own lap.

She grabs his arm and holds it against her stomach. "Stop!"

Time was when he could lift her, flip her over his shoulder, and set her down on the floor behind him. Now she overpowers him with her small body.

"Honestly," she says when he's still, "it's like having a baby again."

He turns away from her and folds his good left arm across his limp right forearm.

"Okay, you win." She sighs. "Let me see what I can do for lunch. But you have to promise you'll eat whatever I serve."

The lesser victory secure, he crosses his heart, pats his lap. *Come here.* She repositions the table in front of him and massages his hand again. As her fingers perform their usual magic, his hand finally relaxes. When she lets go, he starts to spell again. "BEFORE-ANNINA-DIED—"

"I know the story."

"HER-DEAD-MAMMA—"

"Came to visit." She finishes the sentence for him. "The old Italian superstition. I've heard it a thousand times."

Had Nonna really come to Annina as bones? Surely she would have said, "Mamma came to me as bones." But Nonna's appearance hadn't frightened her. She'd told him that night, "I've outgrown the world."

"Outgrown?" he'd said. "*Cara mia*, you're only sixty-one."

He laughs his soundless laugh, remembering the press of her index finger on his lips.

"Hold me," she'd said. When was the last time she'd asked? So he held her as he'd held her when they were newlyweds, her head beneath his chin, her back cupped against his torso. They fell asleep that way, as if they were one body. It wasn't long after that she died.

Rose is whispering now, almost to herself. "Mom was in pain. Her lungs kept filling with fluid." She pinches the bridge of her nose, massaging the vertical lines that worry her forehead.

He touches her free hand and waits.

She looks at him, finally, and says, "You don't have those problems. The doctor says you could live another ten years." She pats his shoulder before she loads the dirty dishes onto the breakfast tray.

He knows what it's like to let go. She doesn't. At the hospital after each stroke, she'd agreed to everything—feeding tube, respirator, resuscitation when his heart failed. His reward for surviving? Flexing his good hand around a rubber ball. Moaning syllables that refuse to form words. Learning to swallow again.

He tries one more time. "NOT-WELL," he spells. "NOT-AFRAI—"

"Enough!" she says, wheeling the table away from him.

The "D" he was reaching for wavers then blurs into the other letters as the board recedes, the letters now just ragged black lines floating above a white field.

"Exercise," she says, placing a pink rubber ball from the night-stand into his left hand and wrapping his fingers around it before she, too, fades through the doorway carrying his breakfast tray.

Vincent can hear Rose calling up the stairs to her husband Frank, "Pop's ready for his bath." He squeezes his fingers around the ball until his knuckles turn white. His left hand trembles again, his right remains irrevocably rigid, the finger-nails digging into the palm's flesh. *These hands,* he thinks, look-ing down at them. *These hands, not my own. These hands guided Rose's hands when I taught her to sew. Pitched a thousand practice hardballs to Vinnie Junior. Laced Annina's fingers as they drifted down the curve of my stomach. These hands, not my own.*

He throws the ball across the bedroom, where it ricochets off the far wall, bounces along the floor, and rolls under the bureau.

*   *   *

With Rose gone, Vincent listens to the sounds that keep him company. He tells time by them. A lone starling muttering qui-etly to itself in the dogwood outside his window. Water sluicing through the pipes in the wall behind him. Children's footsteps echoing above on wooden floors. *6:45,* he thinks. *Not quite 7:00.*

He glances at one of the photographs on his bedside table, his three granddaughters decked out in their Easter bonnets and dresses. The middle child in her lavender dress—her name? her name? Before half his face fell down, she was the one who'd wake with the birds, come to him, and climb on his lap. They'd pull the rolling table over to where both of them could reach it and pretend to play the piano, her fingers resting on his as they walked up and down the edge of the table. Since his last stroke, she only comes when her mother is busy. Even then, she doesn't look at him. He is, to her, a body, if that, a body like a plant, needing to be watered, fed, placed in the sunlight. No lon-ger her Pop-Pop, player of imaginary songs. Today, he couldn't even play an imaginary scale, but oh, if his beautiful, nameless granddaughter could have heard him play the "Tarantella" to Annina's whirling dance, black hair fanned out from her head, face glazed with perspiration, skirt rising and falling in waves around her knees. She's here, in the corner, dancing, and then it's only the bedside table, its cloth skirt falling in sensuous curves around turned cherrywood legs.

He sighs and returns to listening. Through the ceiling, he hears bedsprings creaking. That would be his oldest granddaughter—Kate, yes! Ten-year-old Katy-did! The bedsprings creak again. Lately all Vincent knew of Kate was the scene that unwound each morning outside his window: Kate flying down the steep slope of the front lawn toward the idling school bus, her long ponytail bouncing up and down, her mother ten feet behind waving a brown bag lunch over her head. He'd overheard Kate more than once yell at Rose, both for embarrassing her in front of her busmates and for thinking leftover roast pork and pepper sandwiches were something she'd actually eat for lunch.

Vincent settles his head on the pillow and vows to be nicer to his daughter. He'll eat what she serves. He'll do his hand exercises without being reminded. He won't complain. He sighs, knowing how difficult vows are to keep.

A light breeze again rustles the low branches of the dogwood whose buds are swollen, days from blooming. What will follow are two weeks of spring mornings where the cruciform flowers open and open and open, brilliant white against the green green of spring. In Roccamaro, there were trees like this, white-flowering in mid-spring as he and Annina and her father bent to their work in wooden chairs outside their home, she weaving bridal lace with silk thread, and he and his father-in-law fashioning fine suits of gabardine and cassimere. *The flowers open and open. What were those flowers called, Annina?* She would know. Two weeks later, petals falling, she sweeping them into her palm, the fragrant petals later scattered on the shelves of their chifforobe. He'd find a brown-edged petal in his shirt cuff, hold it to his nose, remember spring.

The trees leaf and shade them. He hums as he sews a sleeve together with fine stitches. She smiles at him from her chair in the doorway's cool dark, touches his hand as he guides the plunging needle through the seam. *The flowers open. What was their name, Annina? Is that, too, forever lost? What if we'd stayed in that doorway stitching and weaving, straight pins and needles, bobbins and pins? Why was it I left you alone all those years? I can't remember leaving. Memory is a dream of...what? Wake and sleep. An argument then silence. Your fist slamming the dining room table. Dinner plates dancing across polished wood. Water trembling in crystal glasses. Why are you crying? Tell me her name! Here's my handkerchief. Dry your tears. Your hand on mine, in the doorway's cool dark, the tickle of your fingertips as you trace the line of my—*

Frank shakes Vincent's arm. "Good morning, Pop," he says.

He hears the bath filling in the next room. *How much time did I just lose?*

Frank pulls back the covers and lifts Vincent from the bed. He can smell a faint trace of Rose's lavender perfume on Frank's skin as his head falls against his son-in-law's bare chest. Frank and Rose together in bed in the early, early morning hours. The thought makes him smile.

Frank carries him into the bathroom as if he's a hollow man, not the flesh-and-blood, two-hundred-pound man of three years ago. He strips off the soiled pajamas, the rubber underwear, and that urine-soaked *thing* that looks like a woman's sanitary napkin, and positions him on the toilet, all without saying another word or looking him in the face *A plant*, Vincent thinks, envisioning a vine unfurling leaf by leaf, twining up toward heaven, roots slowly pulling away from the soil.

"Are you finished?" Frank asks, checking his left wrist, though he isn't wearing a watch.

Vincent shakes his head. Frank breathes out slowly through his teeth. *Who can blame him? So much of the burden falls to Frank—not only caring for me, but soothing his wife.*

Vincent shifts on the toilet seat. "Done?" Frank asks.

This time, Vincent nods, even though he isn't sure he's

finished. Frank wipes his father-in-law, half-carries him to the tub, and helps him down until he's sitting with his back against the cold porcelain. Vincent pushes his good leg against the far end of the tub to prevent his body from slipping forward.

"You need anything else?" Frank asks, sliding a bath tray—soap, a long-handled brush, an open bottle of shampoo, tooth-brush, electric razor—within reach. Vincent makes a circle of his good thumb and index finger, *okay.*

"I'll be back after my shower," Frank says, and disappears through the bathroom door.

Vincent runs the shaver along the thinning stubble of his cheeks and chin, then rubs his hand over his face to check for rough spots. A mirror is suctioned to the tile wall at eye level, but to use it would reveal the dozen raised capillaries threading his face, the age spots scattered like discolored pennies across his cheeks, the drooping right eyelid whose fierce red underside films with cloudy tears. It's enough that his face feels smooth to the touch when he's finished shaving. He wants to be ready. *When Annina comes, she'll kiss me here.* He traces the deep hollow in his left cheek where there's still some feeling.

Releasing himself to the lightness of the bath, he closes his eye. His mind is a darkening sky, edged in a narrowing band of light. He moans out loud to hold ideas in his head:

My granddaughters' names are...Kathleen, Helen, and Grace.
My sister-in-law's name was...Theresa.
When Annina comes...I shall die.

*   *   *

The bathwater's gone lukewarm. Vincent's lower back throbs. *How is it possible I feel anything when nothing works?* His hand begins to slap the water involuntarily. He thinks, inexplicably, of seals, then of the seals he and Rose once saw off the New Jersey shore, crying loudly at the gulls overhead as they beat their flippers against the shallow water. When was that? She's a child, clapping her hands as if watching a show, Vinnie oblivious, firing seashells into the ocean. Annina stands away from them. He tries to pin the flapping hand against the tub with his hip. He slips forward and his hand shoots out, upending the bath tray. The razor flips on when it hits the floor, skitters buzzing across the hard tile, then crashes into the wall and goes quiet.

He fights to stop his slide, but his leg is tired from the prolonged effort of propping himself up. He grasps the handicap bar and pulls. It feels as if he might rip the bar out of the tile wall, but when he looks down, he's barely moved. His leg begins to shake. *How easy to let go, fold my leg under, embrace the water. So many ways to die.* He's halfway down, moaning long strings of O's, *O Dio, O Dio, O Dio.* His body continues down until it's almost horizontal, limbs tucked under each other like a folded shirt. The water closes over his head, his mouth sending bubbles to the surface. He can feel his lungs squeezing shut like an accordion. No worse than choking on the white bean, except the pressure is farther down, in his lungs, not in his windpipe. In the absence of resistance, he inhales a bit of water instead of air. Muffled noises, arms under his arms—he's rising up, floating. The lightness of air instead of the weight of water.

"What the hell?" Frank yells, reaching into the water to pull the white rubber drain plug. "What the hell do you think you're doing?"

Frank pounds on his back. The blows resound off the tile walls. Water sprays out of his mouth. He coughs so hard it feels as if part of his lung is coming out. His gasping for air is a bodily reflex. He tries to reverse the effect, force the air out of his lungs.

The drain sucks the last of the water from the tub. Frank reaches over the edge of the tub, tugs on Vincent's body.

"Damn it, Pop, help me out here. How am I going to explain this to Rose?" Frank's raised voice rings in Vincent's ears.

He squats down and grasps Vincent under the arms. He yanks him almost to a standing position, up and over the rim of the tub. They come to rest sitting on the floor, braced against the bathroom wall. A fine sweat like a rash breaks out over

Frank's face. They're breathing hard, almost in unison. A minute passes, then two.

"I won't tell Rose about this if you promise not to do that again," he says at last, looking into Vincent's slack face. "Can you give me a sign here? Give me a sign. Are you okay, Pop?"

The bathroom door bursts open. "What's all the yelling?" Rose asks.

Frank turns to Vincent, then to her. "Everything's fine," he says.

But she's staring at her father. He stares back. "What happened, Pop?"

Without taking his good eye off her, Vincent drums his fingers on his naked thigh. She takes his cue, disappears into the bedroom, while Frank calls after her, "Pop's foot must have slipped. I took too long upstairs. Katie was forever in the shower."

Frank turns to Vincent and whispers, "She doesn't have to know."

Rose returns with the alphabet board, holds it horizontally between her hands, and kneels down in front of her father. He's shivering, his teeth clacking open and shut, but he doesn't motion for a towel. He places his left hand on the board, water dripping on the wood. He points to "D"—

"He's okay, Rose," Frank says.

—to "R"—

"Everything's okay now," Frank says.

—to "O," then "W"—

"I don't think he could have drowned in eight inches of water. For Christ's sake, Pop." Frank rakes a hand through his hair.

—and finally "N."

"Is this the first time?" Her question is for either man to answer.

Frank nods, but Vincent simply stares at her.

"If that's the way you want it," she says, her face flushed from fighting not to raise her voice. "We won't leave you alone, even for a minute."

The tremor in his left hand is increasing, but either because he's shivering so violently or because Rose is distracted, she doesn't notice.

"Get him dressed," she says, "and put him by the living room window." She throws a towel at her father's lap and turns to leave without waiting for a reply from either of them.

*　　*　　*

Days pass. Days pass. *How many days have passed?*

He resists the urge to open his eye, but he feels the shadow of light. He could pass his whole life down in the dark roots of his body, the light of smell and sound and touch above. Mown grass. The lone starling calling. The living room sheers billowing, drifting across his face. A fluttering white nightgown. *What day? Tuesday? Friday?* He savors the fabric's caress, the slant of morning sunlight warming his body. Annina's eyes are heavy-lidded from sleep. She bends to kiss him on the forehead, on each cheek, on his mouth. His two good hands come up to meet hers, pull her into his lap. *Vieni, carissima.*

"Rose, hon? Where are you, Rose?" Frank calls.

She appears in the kitchen doorway, wiping her hands on a dish towel. Frank crosses to where she's standing, kisses her on the cheek, runs his finger under her chin. She pushes him away, smiling. "You're late for work."

Then the screen door slams shut, and a car engine roars to life, fades away.

I heard them through the wall, Annina. How many days ago? 'It would've been better if you'd let him choke!' Did you hear?

Rose hovers over the stereo. A record drops onto the turntable, a faint click as the arm lifts, shifts, falls. The needle plays air until it finds the first groove in the black vinyl. Four dark notes, *da-da-da-dum,* loud as drums. *How many days have passed?* Rose is mending. *How many days in this body? Tell me, Rose, how long?* His eye is open. Rose is mending. *What happened to our conversation?* He waits for her

107

usual running monologue. *Da-da-da-dum. Four dark notes.* Calling violin, answering bass. He coughs and steals a sideways glance at her, but she is mending. He waits for a response. *Perhaps if I were a plant, she'd water me? If I were a plant, she'd know that I was dying.*

The low music creates a pleasant vibration in his head, night notes echoing. He hums, tries to keep his eye open. She is mending. *Did you hear, Annina? Did you hear the screen door slamming? Did you stay awake all night? Did you hear Frank's footfalls on the stairs? Up and down he went, wondering if she'd come home. A door opening, a door closing. Did they go to bed afterward? Did she turn from him in bed? You turned from me in bed. Your black hair falling like a curtain. Your black hair like a curtain falling into the long silence.* The fullness of late morning light, the thrum in his teeth. *The long silence. The moment our two bodies. The comfort of Theresa's body so long ago. Before. Before you came to America.*

The sheer white curtains catch the stream of sunlight and fling it into the room. He taps his left hand in four-four time against the wheelchair, drumming to stay awake. *The murmur in my head, the murmur in my head.* It travels down his neck, spreads to his arms and spine. The flash of silver needles in the sunlight. She is mending. *She is mending. Why did we never speak of comfort? The long silence of those years? Is that the reason for your silence? I hear dark notes, loud as drums. Four dark notes, loud as drums. Calling violin, answering bass. Violins calling. Nothing answering.*

His left hand jerks suddenly, no longer in time to the music. He stretches his hand, resumes tapping, but the tremor grows more erratic. The vibration travels up his arm, becomes waves. *Waves on the ocean and seals, inexplicably seals, and Annina turned away from me. Her hair falling like silence. The muffled click of a needle against a thimble. Four dark notes, flashes of light then dark. Swimming up from the dark, Theresa. No, not Theresa, but her bones. Theresa's face. A body of bones. Rose!* His muffled cry, an underwater sound.

His tongue thickens, expanding to fill his whole mouth. *Rose!* rising in the air like a bubble. Something presses on the soft palette of his temple, circles around the back of his head, moves across his eyes like a blindfold pulled tight. He lifts his left hand to remove it, but this hand has also frozen in place. The pressure in his forehead turns into pain so intense that both of his eyes water. He forces his left eye open. Through a glaze of tears, he sees Rose pull a tufted footrest, Annina's old sewing stool, toward her and rummage inside for notions. *Rose!*

His moaning causes her to look up.

Please, Rose.

"You okay, Pop?" She crosses to where he's sitting and wipes his tears with her shirt.

His head grows heavy with music, the warmth of her skin through the fabric of her clothing, her hand on his shoulder. *Annina, forgive me.*

"What is it, Pop?"

His vision clears, and he finds it's Rose, only Rose, standing there.

* * *

He wakes to the odor of sauteed pancetta. *Spaghetti carbonara,* he thinks, his mouth watering involuntarily. He swallows hard, trying to stifle his body's natural reflexes.

"Are you ready for lunch?" Rose asks. Without waiting for an answer, without giving him a chance to help push, she wheels him into the kitchen. "I kept my promise, not that you deserve it after what you pulled this morning."

The drowning moment, he thinks. *So it's the same day, whatever day it was this morning.*

She ladles pasta, dripping with a creamy sauce, from a steaming pot into a large ceramic bowl. With two sharp knives, she slices up his spaghetti, then bows. "Lunch," she says, placing the bowl in front of him, "is served."

He sniffs, wrinkles his nose in the rising mist.

"Don't start," she says, putting equal emphasis on each word.

He considers her face—the deepening worry lines, the gray shadows in the pouches beneath her eyes.

"Please," she says, more gently, touching his arm.

He doesn't move.

"You don't want to get better? What would Mom say if she saw you now, how you aren't even trying? It's good. Just like you asked for. I left it a little chunky so you could taste the spaghetti and the pancetta."

He feels sorry for her. His body is changing, even as he sits with her. He'll die soon, with or without her approval. He thought earlier, by the open window, Annina there. But no. He takes a spoonful of carbonara. She pats his hand. He tongues the pasta into the back of his mouth, and, focusing his mind on the task of swallowing, tries to ignore the shards pricking the back of his throat. *She's feeding me silver needles.*

"Good?" she asks.

He nods. He watches her twirl a heaping forkful of creamy spaghetti in her soup spoon, then lift it to her mouth, chew, and swallow. "Remember when Vinnie and I were young, and Mom used to make us drink that frothy orange juice from frozen concentrate?" She taps her fork on his bowl.

Pretending to hurry the cooling, he pushes his soupy pasta from one side to the other, scoops another spoonful, and looks up at her.

She smiles at him, then twirls another forkful. "I'd ask her what she put in it, and she'd swear, 'it's just I put it in the blender.' That stuff was vile. You know what the secret ingredient was?"

He stares at her mutely. It's an effort even to think.

"Raw egg. She said it was good for us. It's a wonder she didn't kill Vinnie and me with salmonella!" She eats the forkful and glances out the kitchen window. "Vinnie won't come home, you know. He can't stand to see you like this."

She turns back to him. He's given up even the pretense of eating, the taste of metal strong in his mouth.

"C'mon, Pop, you promised." She puts down her fork, fills his spoon, and touches her father's lips with it. "Here you go!" she says, pushing the food into his mouth.

A gurgling sound comes from the back of his throat. He grabs his neck with one hand.

"No you don't," she says. "Please don't."

He squeezes his eye shut.

"Really, Pop," she says. "It's good."

She eats what's left on his spoon, then shovels spoonful after spoonful of his pasta into her mouth. "Please," she says, velvety sauce dripping from her lips. "Is it because the pieces are too big? Is it?"

He begins to gag. What little he's managed to eat comes up and spreads over the cloth napkin tucked into his collar.

"Okay," she says, swallowing hard. "Okay, okay, okay."

She grabs both bowls and throws them into the sink, where they shatter against the porcelain. Some of the pasta runs down the drain. She pushes broken ceramic and spaghetti into the garbage disposal and flips the switch. For a minute, screeching fills the room as the disposal tries to digest the mess. A scent like burning rubber wafts up from the drain, then silence.

Her back to him, she stands at the sink, her shoulders rising and falling. She inhales deeply as if the air around her has suddenly become insubstantial.

He wheels himself slowly, single-handedly, left wheel then right, left then right, over to the sink. Her head is down, her dark hair loose over her shoulders. *Annina.* So many days spent in silence. He's forgotten, exactly, the *letting-go moment.* How would life have been different if he'd stayed in the ladder-back chair, its legs like tendrils rooting him to earth, Annina and her father and he making wedding clothes, the same clothes, over and over, stitches and needles, bobbins and pins, moving so fast everything begins to blur, all light and no substance, slicing air into slivers of time, the slivers drifting down, layering like petals falling to earth?

Would it have been so different, carissima?

The woman turns slowly, arms folded across her chest. Her face is wet. Strands of hair cling to her cheeks.

Forgive me.

They stare at each other across the narrow space separating them. Without looking down, Vincent forces the thumb of his left hand around to the index finger, lifts his hand slightly, and raises his left eyebrow to show he's asking a question. *Okay?*

He takes the woman's right hand in his left, forms her fingers into the same gesture, and waits for her to give him what he wants.

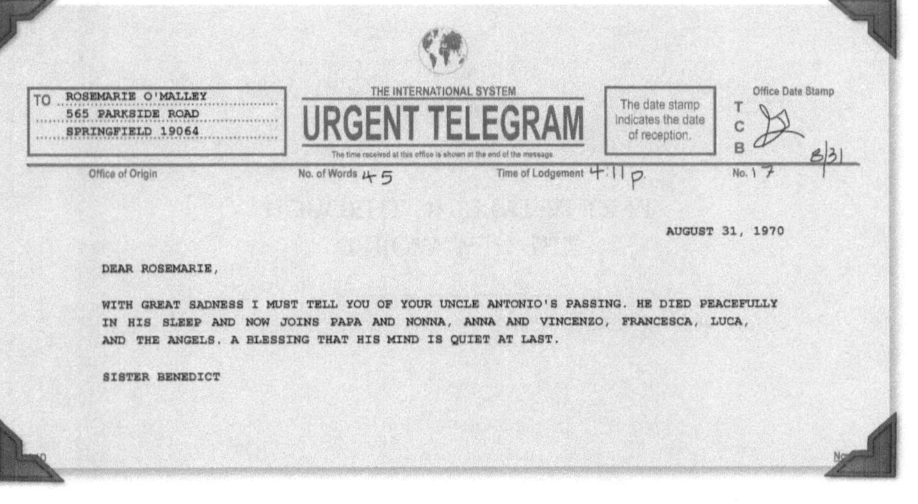

THE INTERNATIONAL SYSTEM
URGENT TELEGRAM
The time received at this office is shown at the end of the message.
The date stamp indicates the date of reception.
Office Date Stamp
T C B
TO ROSEMARIE O'MALLEY
565 PARKSIDE ROAD
SPRINGFIELD 19064
Office of Origin
No. of Words 45
Time of Lodgement 4:11 p.
No. 17
8/31
AUGUST 31, 1970
DEAR ROSEMARIE,
WITH GREAT SADNESS I MUST TELL YOU OF YOUR UNCLE ANTONIO'S PASSING. HE DIED PEACEFULLY
IN HIS SLEEP AND NOW JOINS PAPA AND NONNA, ANNA AND VINCENZO, FRANCESCA, LUCA,
AND THE ANGELS. A BLESSING THAT HIS MIND IS QUIET AT LAST.
SISTER BENEDICT

PART IV: FALLING THROUGH THE NEW WORLD

CLOSING TIME

Arriving at the New Jersey shore always had a strange effect on Kate. After she passed over the two bridges that led into Cape May, she rolled down the car windows to breathe in salt air and listen to the strident *keow keow* of swarming seagulls. A peculiar sense of freedom came over her. She could shed her life back in Philadelphia, if only for the two weeks she spent with her extended family in the beachfront Victorian they rented every year.

She'd notified her clients that she'd be out-of-office, though it seemed to her that the whole world took off the last two weeks of August. Well, almost everybody. Her husband, James, begged off the first week at the shore—he was on the verge of closing a big commercial real estate deal that he'd been working on the past year. Or so he said. Kate knew that spending time with her family wasn't the vacation of his dreams. In any case, he promised to join her that evening.

On the afternoon of his impending arrival, Kate and her mother, Rose, left the beach early to shop for new dresses to wear to O'Hara's that evening. It was their Friday night tradition of drinking and singing along to Irish songs and dancing to soft rock tunes and swing music.

"Shopping," Rose liked to say, "is God's antidote to men."

As they walked along Beach Avenue admiring the clothes that hung in shop windows—sunflower-colored halters, turquoise tube tops, and fuchsia dresses with plunging necklines— Kate couldn't help but think how different they were compared to what she could buy in the suburban shopping malls west of Philadelphia. They passed a teenaged couple, hands in each other's back pockets, tongue-kissing as they leaned against a light pole strung with leaping dolphins. The couple's posture reminded Kate of the first kiss she and James had shared. After turning over the "closed" sign and locking the door of the pizza shop where she earned her way through college, she'd pressed him against a wall. They'd practically eaten each other's tongues, the effect of his desire digging into her hip.

"You're awfully quiet," Rose said.

Kate sighed. "Am I?"

"You'll feel better when James gets here. I'm sure it's not that exciting being on vacation with Dad and Uncle Vinnie and Grace."

"It's not that, Mom. It's just...it's just James and me. We're going through a rough patch. He's working around the clock, and I'm hardly ever home. I'm getting sick of traveling for business and smiling at my clients when all I want to do is tell them to get lost."

They paused in front of a store displaying an assortment of whirligigs twirling in the breeze. A young boy was amusing himself by pressing the flimsy blades of one colorful toy, making it stop and start at will. Kate knelt and mimicked the boy's play with another of the spinners.

"Where's your mom?" Rose asked the boy.

"Inside," he said. "She told me to wait here."

Just then, the boy's mother appeared. "Let's go, Timmy," she said, taking his hand and pulling him along. He turned once and waved at Kate, who waved back.

"Some people," Rose said, shaking her head. "You know, Kate, you and James should be thinking about children. If you don't hurry, you'll be too old to enjoy them."

"I'm working on it, Mom."

"In California and Texas, you're working on it?"

"What am I supposed to do—trick him into having children?"

"It's been done before. Sometimes men don't know what

they want."

"That's your advice?" Kate asked. But she wondered if her mother was right. When they talked about having children, James had one excuse after another for waiting. It always boiled down to money. He'd grown up in a family that was always one paycheck away from foreclosure. No matter how much they put aside, though, it was never enough. It's not as if they hadn't discussed the matter before getting married. The Catholic Church made them promise to have children during their mandatory Pre-Cana preparation. Even back then, James had hedged. Out of the priest's earshot, he suggested that thirty was a good age to start a family. Thirty seemed impossibly far away eight years ago. And now they *were* thirty.

Kate slowed down in front of a swimwear shop. The headless mannequins sported swimsuits she'd dreamed of wearing in her teens, but her mother would never allow her to buy. She tried to imagine herself in the white crocheted two-piece bikini in the display window. She'd been slender enough in college, never thin, but curved in the right places. It wasn't until she was older, looking back from the vantage point of several years of marriage, that she'd realized the power women had over men, the power she once had. In truth, she'd been afraid of men, afraid that she'd end up like her sister Helen.

"Your old friend Elizabeth Newberry? She's going through a divorce right now. Married only six years."

"I know, Mom."

"Turns out he wanted kids and she didn't. Her mother is ashamed to come to church now because of the scandal."

"Honestly, no one thinks like that anymore." Kate tapped on the window of another shop featuring a white halter dress. "Can we pop in here?"

Rose wrinkled her nose, then shrugged. Inside the store, she waited while Kate ducked in a changing room and came out modeling the dress.

"Don't you think that's—"

"You want grandkids?" Kate asked.

Rose smiled. "Point taken. Let me treat you."

"Really, Mom, that's not necessary."

"I insist!" she said, removing a credit card from a wallet overstuffed with them.

"What about you?"

She laughed. "Nothing here for mature women."

Kate asked the salesclerk for a bag to carry the outfit she'd been wearing. Outside again, they crossed Beach Avenue and walked along the concrete promenade, a gentle wind blowing in from the Atlantic, ruffling Kate's new dress.

"Do you think they'll return the wedding gifts?" Rose asked.

"Who?"

"The Newberrys. I mean, six years? How do you know what you want after only six years? It's a disgrace. The Church says for better, for worse. Why bother getting married if you don't take the vow seriously?"

"I'm sure if they knew they'd be getting divorced, they wouldn't have gotten married in the first place."

"Sometimes all that keeps a marriage together *is* the vow."

"Can I needlepoint that on a pillow?"

"Don't be sarcastic. Dad and I have had our ups and downs."

"If you call a nervous breakdown a down."

"That was a long time ago." Her mother turned toward the ocean as she spoke, her voice so soft that the thunder of waves crashing against the rocks beneath them nearly drowned out her words. "Eight years of marriage don't qualify you to judge my life. You can't possibly understand what Helen did to me—nineteen and pregnant! After all those years of Catholic school, no less."

Rose stopped suddenly and took a seat on an empty bench facing the ocean. Kate sat beside her, the silence washing over them. They'd had this discussion a hundred times before. Understanding each other was like trying to fill a balloon with a pinprick hole. They were from two different generations of Catholic women. Rose staunchly believed heaven was her ultimate reward for persevering on earth. Their pastor, Father Isaac, used to drone on from the pulpit every Sunday about the sacrifices and suffering of earthly life being necessary to earn the perfect happiness of heaven. Back then, Kate would steal sideways glances at her mother, mimic her rigid posture, her white-gloved hands folded in her lap, the circle of a white lace veil bobby-pinned to her hair (even after the head covering was no longer required by the Church) as her head dipped at every mention of the word *Jesus*. Kate couldn't remember the last time she'd been to Mass other than the obligatory posturing with her family the previous Sunday at Lady Star of the Sea.

Was her mother's nervous breakdown an example of the suffering to which the old pastor referred? They rarely talked about what happened a decade ago—1975—when Kate was twenty. What Kate recalled about that summer was coming home from her sophomore year at Villanova—the Catholic college her mother had insisted upon for her and Helen, as if a Catholic college might ward off any trespass into sin—and rocking her mother while she sobbed in their darkened living room. What she remembered was the loneliness of the bedroom she'd shared with Helen after her mother sent Helen away. Born only a year apart, they'd been inseparable growing up—trading gossip about boys, practicing the art of makeup, and falling in love with David Cassidy. It was Kate who showed Helen how to use a tampon. When Rose found Tampax in the bathroom vanity, she confronted Kate, waving the box in the air and saying, "Virgins can't use tampons. What are you trying to do here, Kate?" Then she flushed the cardboard tubes one by one down the toilet.

Later, she and Helen would joke "only sluts use tampons" every time they bought them in secret and hid them in a locked "treasure chest" they kept in their closet.

Helen lost her virginity to a freshman she was dating and swore her sister to secrecy. When Rose found out Helen was pregnant, she sent her to a home for unwed mothers in upstate Pennsylvania. Abortion, though legal, was out of the question.

Kate spent her breaks during that year listening to her mother's tirades about Kate's failed responsibility to her sister, as if tampons had somehow given Helen the idea for sex.

"No one has to know," her mother whispered into the womb of the living room.

The two women had sat long enough in silence people-watching and enjoying the perfect afternoon weather that the waves no longer quite reached the wall of rocks below the promenade. As the breeze picked up and the air grew chillier, Rose stood and smoothed the wrinkles in her skirt. "We should be getting back," she said.

They walked along the promenade, past the arcades and the convention center, Morrow's Nut House, all the old familiar boardwalk concessions, stopping only to sample fudge held out on a tray by a young girl whose job it was to lure passersby into the shop with tiny squares of the candy.

They'd almost reached the house when Rose said, "You know, Kate, it wouldn't kill you to apologize. You owe me that much."

Kate looked at her mother's face, the defeat she read there the result of the hundreds of concessions the woman had made in her life just to keep moving forward, trying not to fall, a baby perpetually taking first steps.

"Okay," she said. "I'm sorry, Mom," though she wasn't sure what she was apologizing for.

*   *   *

When Kate and Rose arrived at the house, the sun was angling down, gilding the waves as they raced to shore. Grace, Kate's youngest sister, was sitting on the front porch, cross-legged on a hanging chair, a thick book in her lap.

"So, I guess you're not going dancing with us?" Rose said, eyeing Grace's outfit, a ratty Barnard College sweatshirt and frayed jean shorts.

"I'd rather die than go dancing." She looked at her mother

over the top of her wire-rimmed glasses. "All that sweat, and bodies pushing together."

"God forbid!" Kate said. She set down her shopping bag, then twirled around in her new dress. The white halter top cupped snugly around her breasts, cinched at her waist, and flared out at her hips.

Grace scowled at her sister and resumed reading her book. "Well?" Kate said.

"Well, what?" She looked up, finger-combing her wet hair. "The dress?"

"You want me to tell you you're thirty trying to look eighteen again? That dress has 'screw me' written all over it."

"Screw *you*, baby sister."

"Mary Kathleen! Grace Marie!"

"Oh, Mom, lighten up." Grace shot a glance at Kate, mouthing the words *Mary Kathleen* and *Grace Marie*. "We're grown-ups now."

Kate wondered when Grace had lost her sense of humor. When she first brought James home, her little sister had shadowed them like a faithful hound. Now she had no time for *boys*. She had chosen Barnard over her mother's objections, paying her way on student loans and minimum-wage jobs, so what could her mother do? By then Rose had given up on the idea that a Catholic education protected her girls from anything.

"You don't hear *me* using language like that. Or Dad or Uncle Vinnie, for that matter. And they're men."

"So there are different rules for men?" she asked.

"What don't I do?" Kate's father, Frank, asked. He was carrying two armfuls of sand chairs and had an assortment of beach towels draped around his neck. He dropped the chairs to either side of his legs and mopped his forehead with one of the brightly striped towels. Vinnie came up behind her father, wielding a beach umbrella like a sword.

"Dad, don't be so clueless. She was yelling at *us* this time," Grace said.

"Enough, all of you," Rose said. "What kept you guys?"

Frank looked down at the chairs as if they were the obvious answer to her question.

Vinnie broke the silence. "The beach was perfect. No clouds, no wind. We hated to leave." He nodded in the direction of the sea.

"We told you dinner at seven. It's almost seven now."

Frank busied himself hosing the sand off the chairs, methodically rinsing each one from the top down.

"We thought you told us eight," Vinnie said.

Rose crossed her arms. "Eight? We never eat that late."

"That's what we thought you said," Frank said.

"If you listened to me—"

"Mom, James isn't here yet. Does it matter?" Kate skipped down the porch stairs to help her father, setting the wet chairs in the waning sun to dry. "We can't leave until he gets here."

"Nice dress," Vinnie said.

Kate smiled. "Thanks for noticing."

"Where is James, anyway?" Rose asked. "He told us six."

"I heard on the radio that there was a massive pile-up on the expressway. He's probably stuck in traffic," Grace said.

"Great! We'll never get out of here." Rose threw up her hands, palms outward, as if she were surrendering. "I have an announcement. We're leaving here in an hour. We're going to dinner and dancing at O'Hara's. If you want to come, hurry up and get ready. If you don't, you're on your own."

Kate went upstairs to her room and locked the door behind her. She took off the halter dress and draped it over a chair. Standing naked except for her underwear, she looked at herself in the mirror. Her brown hair and square face were those of her father, but her body was beginning to resemble her mother's—the same wide hips and large, rounded breasts—the result of gaining twenty pounds since her wedding. James never complained, but it had been a long time since he'd told her she was beautiful.

Was it always that after marriage, the present overwhelmed the past and planning for the future usurped the pleasure of the present? What was the point of the pretense her mother created for the outside world? It was so difficult to pretend all the time. She wondered how her mother did it. Beautiful clothes, credit card bills paid with credit card checks from other accounts. Her first grandchild, Helen's *illegitimate* daughter, raised by an anonymous couple in an unknown location. Yet her mother liked to brag on the phone to her best friend, Cecelia, how Helen was the assistant to some big Hollywood star. Kate knew the truth of her sister's studio apartment in a marginal Los Angeles neighborhood and the doggie bags she took home every time Kate treated her to dinner on her expense account. Helen still keeping secrets, begging Kate, "Don't tell Mom." It was all Kate could do not to rip the phone out of her mother's hand and tell Cecelia the truth. And now Kate was supposed to have the first *legitimate* grandchild, and on her mother's schedule?

The doorknob rattled. "Kate, it's me." It was James.

"Just a sec," she said. Kate slipped on her new dress and opened the door. When she saw the dark circles under his eyes and the sweat staining the underarms of his wrinkled button-down, she refrained from scolding him for being late.

"I was just taking a nap before dinner," she said, pulling him into the room and closing the door. "How was the drive?"

"A nightmare. Bumper-to-bumper on the Atlantic City Expressway. There were, like, ten smashed-up cars in the passing lane, and cops everywhere, and EMTs. If I'd left the office ten minutes sooner, I might have been one of them." He stretched out on the double bed, laced his hands under his head, and closed his eyes.

"James?"

He forced his eyes open. "Yeah?"

Kate spun around. Her dress flared out from her narrowed waist and curled around her legs. "What do you think?"

"Of what?" he asked. "Oh, the dress. Don't you think it's, I mean, not really you?"

Kate stopped spinning, awkwardly adjusting the straps that held her breasts in place. "Mom helped pick it out. She wants grandchildren."

He laughed, and his laughter was infectious. She sat down on the bed and laughed with him until she had to wipe tears from her eyes. Then she kissed him, and he kissed her back and ran his hand up her waist and under the halter top. They lay back on the bed.

Just then through the wall, they could hear her parents' bickering in the adjacent bedroom.

"If you'd listened to me, we'd be there by now," Rose was saying.

"Someone had to bring the stuff up from the beach," Frank said. "We'll get there when we get there. Nobody's going to *starve*."

"You know I hate waiting," Rose said.

Kate shrugged. "Same old, same old."

"Has it been like this all week?" he asked. Her parents' petty squabbling was one reason she knew he hadn't hurried to the shore. Their quarreling felt like a disease that penetrated her skin whenever she and James were around her parents for too long.

Through the wall, they heard a closet door slam.

"I didn't hear you," Frank said.

"So get a hearing aid."

"I don't need..."

The rest of Frank's words were drowned out by Rose's blow dryer. Frank was hard of hearing, a consequence of playing drums in a swing band in the forties. His refusal to get a hearing aid was only partly vanity. The greater part, Kate thought, was that her father endured the loss of smaller pieces of his life so that he wouldn't have to let go of something larger.

The blow dryer shut off in the next room, and Rose's voice cut through the sudden silence. "—last time I'm telling you!"

Kate punched the wall and said, "Mom, stop yelling at Dad or we'll leave, I swear to God!"

In the next room, the voices lowered to muffled whispering.

She turned to James. "Look, I know you're tired. I know you'd rather stay here. But it's Friday night, and you know the drill."

"O'Hara's, right?" He sighed. "Can we at least be back at a reasonable hour?"

Kate settled her cheek against his chest. "I promise."

*   *   *

It was midnight, two hours before closing time, and O'Hara's was shoulder-to-shoulder, wall-to-wall. The band was taking a break, and the piano man who filled the interludes was in the middle of "When Irish Eyes Are Smiling." Kate's parents were slow-dancing on the mostly empty dance floor, while Kate, James, and Vinnie sat at the bar. Her uncle was singing low to the song, his voice like poured molasses, rich and thick and dark.

Smoke stung Kate's eyes and hazed the air. Her contacts caused the dim globes over the bar to bleed fuzzy halos. All around her, women leaned their heads into men's cigarette lighters—middle-aged women in dresses cut too low, the scent of coconut sunblock and Johnson's baby oil rising from their skin. Faint traces of frosted pink gloss stained their lips and cigarettes. Dried salt crystals shone on the sun-bleached hairs of darkened arms. A woman in a strapless red dress, dipping one foot to the music, slid down in her chair and blew smoke to the ceiling. A slow fan stirred the smoke, sliced it to pieces. Beyond the barroom, cards were shuffled, plastic chips clicked into a pile. At the pool table, the cue ball danced over green felt and broke ten bright balls to the corners, the sharp crack an accent to the burr of forced laughter.

Kate was on her third vodka tonic, the first two having gone down like soda. The vodka made her feel as if she'd been bound up like a package and someone had taken a knife to the string. She tried to catch James's eye in the mirror that angled overhead behind the bar, but every time she looked up, he looked away, nursing the neck of an empty Heineken bottle.

She turned to her uncle and sang along with him, "When Irish eyes are happy, all the world seems bright and gay..." How could a song with words like *happy* and *gay* always fill her with sadness? Maybe it was the drinking, or the longing in her uncle's voice.

"...sure they steal your heart away." Vinnie leaned into Kate as he sang the last words to her.

"You're insane," she said, smiling.

He raised an index finger to the bartender. "I'll have another, and refresh this handsome young couple's drinks while you're at it."

"Sure thing," the bartender said, looking over Vinnie's head to Kate. She mouthed, "We're walking," and the bartender nodded and set another round in front of them.

Across the bar, Kate noticed two men sit down on stools abandoned by a young couple who'd spent several minutes sucking the alcohol off each other's tongues. The men were tanned, and the older one had a ribbon of gray running through jet-black hair. The younger man was blond and thin, his face creased with sunstruck wrinkles. They waved at the bartender, obviously regulars, and the bartender set a couple of drafts in front of them.

Kate saw her uncle watching them. She thought of her much-younger Uncle Vinnie pulling up in the driveway of their suburban Philadelphia colonial in his Mercedes convertible, a chocolate lab panting in the passenger seat. Her mother had told her long ago that Vinnie acted as if he were a painting one lived inside of. Here was something she and her mother could agree on—her uncle was like a museum piece that people admired from afar but never thought to inspect up close. How did he live and eat and breathe? Was his heart made heavy by the weight of pretending to be something he was not? *Heaven is its own reward*, Kate thought. But how much of one's life did her mother expect people to give up in its pursuit? And of course her mother would never admit to the obvious about her uncle.

Kate turned to James. "Ready to dance?"

"Not yet."

"If you drink many more of those, you won't be able to stand up."

James stood and spread his arms. "See? No problem." He polished off his beer and tugged at her arm. "Let's get out of here."

She pulled away from him and shouted over the music, "I want to dance. I'm not leaving until we dance." The deep-throated, up-tempo clarinet of the band's "In the Mood" sang over the band's amplifiers. "C'mon, I'll lead. This is one of my old-timey favorites."

"I don't want to make a fool of myself."

"I don't care how you dance. Please."

He sat down again, hunched over the bar, and spun his empty beer bottle. The gesture called to mind their first nights together when, alone in his dorm room, they played spin-the-bottle. They'd spent hours on the game he'd probably long since forgotten, followed by the awkward groping that she remembers as the sweetest touching of her life—her hair stuck in his mouth, her arm caught under his back after he fell asleep and she afraid to wake him by moving it.

She reached out and caught the bottle mid-spin. "Who's watching? Tell me. Who? Half the people in here are drunk out of their minds and the other half are on the dance floor."

"Why don't you ask your uncle? He's a good dancer."

"Because I want to dance with you." She cuddled his arm and the soft skin of her breast squeezed against his forearm.

He stood up again and said, "Let's go."

She shook her head, turned away from him, and put her face sideways on the bar. The music vibrated through the wood and throbbed in her cheek. She had no wish to hurry back to the double bed she and James would share just so he could fall asleep, and she'd spend the rest of the night listening to him breathe and thinking about those smashed-up cars on the expressway.

Vinnie turned to Kate. "You okay?"

"I think I've had enough to drink," she said, lifting her head slightly. Her uncle's face swam in front of her, briefly, as the music shifted into a waltz. "Wanna dance?"

Vinnie offered his niece his hand. "My pleasure," he said, and shouted to James, "Save our seats."

He guided her to an empty space next to where her parents were dancing. She put one hand in her uncle's and the other on his shoulder and let him lead her in a waltz she didn't recognize. She watched her parents over her uncle's shoulder, moving in perfect time to the music. Frank turned Rose out in a fancy promenade. She had her hand on her hip and her head tilted down, a half-smile on her lips. They were good dancers, Kate had to admit.

Her father had taught her to dance when she was five. He'd stack a pile of 33s on the turnstile spindle and she'd wait the extra beats for the needle to drop and slide along the opening groove while her heart raced and she inhaled her father's musky Old Spice and then over the speakers of the console stereo she'd hear the scratchy sound of songs from the forties—Glenn Miller, Benny Goodman, Tommy Dorsey—and she'd place her feet on her father's shoes and he'd start with a slow dip and the first steps and she'd laugh and lose the beat and he was extremely patient with her and waited for her to stop laughing and then he'd murmur the beat under his breath, *one-slide step-three-four* for a fox-trot or *step-step-step/step* for a jitterbug, pull her forward and release her, and they'd dance for what seemed like hours to the faraway music played by big band musicians like Glenn Miller who'd long since died in airplane crashes or whatever and she remembers loving her father and wanting to protect him from her mother, from all the nagging and perfecting, from the struggle of their daily life together.

The song ended and everyone clapped. "Thank you," Kate said to her uncle.

"I'm going to ask for our song," he said, and winked at her. She knew the song he meant, "I'll Take You Home Again, Kathleen." Another Friday night tradition. The band segued into a fox-trot, and Kate watched as her uncle danced his way solo over to the piano man, who was setting up in preparation for the end of the band's final set. He waved dollar bills in the air and placed them ceremoniously in the brandy snifter the pianist used for tips.

The woman in the strapless red dress was dancing with a man Kate knew wasn't her husband. The faint white tan line on her left ring finger gave her away. She imagined the woman's children sleeping off sand and salt and sea air—a natural blond son whose bowl-cut fell into his face as he snored gently and a daughter who slept with her arms thrown out as if ready to embrace the world—children Kate could have loved. She imagined the woman's husband had earlier told his wife that he was too tired to drive down to the shore just for the weekend. She imagined him sitting in a restaurant bar in downtown Philadelphia, unwinding after a long week, drinking and watching women pass by on their way to a table in the dining room.

Kate hugged herself and swayed to the brass and slow woodwinds of "Moonlight Serenade." A stranger tapped Kate on the shoulder, a man tanned from long days in the sun.

"Would you like to dance, or do you prefer to dance with yourself?" the man asked.

"Aah," she said. "I really shouldn't."

"That guy you were dancing with is old enough to be your father."

"Actually, he's my uncle." She glanced over at James, who was watching her.

"I'd love to dance," she said, and before the man had a chance to move away, she placed her left arm on his shoulder and grasped his other hand in her right. The gold of her wedding band flashed in the mirrored lights above the dance floor. "I'm Kate."

"Michael," the man said, and pulled her to him. The music transitioned into "What a Wonderful World," a song that should have made Kate feel happy but again provoked a kind of wistful melancholy. She moved into him, resting her chin on his shoulder. She noticed that her parents had stopped dancing, saw her mother whisper in her father's ear and push him toward them, saw her father resist her mother's urging and stand his ground and watch his daughter dance as gracefully as he'd taught her years ago.

The woman in the red dress made her way over to James, bent to his ear, and led him to the dance floor. He looked over at Kate, then pulled the woman toward him, rested his hand low on her back, and danced to the band's final song of the night, "Endless Love." As the last strains of the song faded, he nodded to Kate and left the bar.

Kate considered following him out into the summer night—*I should follow him*, she thought—to salvage what was left of a once promising evening. But then the piano man played the opening notes of *her* song as Vinnie danced his way over to her. *I'll take you home again, Kathleen*, the piano man sang to the four-beat melody, *across the ocean wild and wide, to where your heart has ever been.* Vinnie turned an imaginary partner in his arms, joining in the chorus loud and slow as he went. *Oh! I will take you back, Kathleen, to where your heart will feel no pain. And when the fields are fresh and green, I will take you to your home again!* Each note shone separately, holding itself in the air, shimmering like light as it breaks on waves. *Where laughs the little silver stream beside your mother's humble cot, and brightest rays of sunshine gleam, there all your grief will be forgot.*

Kate's eyes watered as her uncle moved toward her. Neither of their lives had turned out as planned. What was that old saying? Man proposes, God disposes? She knew that he'd long ago resigned himself to life inside the portrait, the "confirmed bachelor" who, according to her mother, had just never met the right woman.

"Last call," the bartender cried.

Kate gestured for her uncle to join her and Michael. The piano man segued into the final number of the night, singing

"Over in Killarney, many years ago." The three held hands and danced round and round like children in a game of Ring Around the Rosie. *Too-ra-loo-ra-loo-ral, Too-ra-loo-ra-li, Too-ra-loo-ra-loo-ral,* they chorused. *Nonsense words,* she thought, but she had to admit they were comforting, as lullabies should be. She felt herself unwinding like the unwinding from a twist in the jitterbug or the long promenade in the middle of a waltz, the stepping away from your partner, away and away, until you reach the farthest point in the arc you trace on the dance floor, and when your partner tries to pull you gently back, you let go, keep spinning outward, turning and turning in ever-widening circles.

A SONG IN ORDINARY TIME

Kate has come to Spoleto in August, when the town empties and its residents flee to the sea or the mountains as a respite from the summer heat. Returning once again to the country her grandparents abandoned, she thinks she might finally have reached the end of something. She's fled too, asked her husband, James, for a separation to think about their past, their present, their future. Last year, she'd done the dramatic—resigned from her job before telling him, thinking that act would force him into a decision to have children. All it had caused was an argument that seems to have lasted the past year without a resolution.

She likes the emptiness of Italy in August. Heat envelops her as she sits under the cool shade of blackthorns on one of the weather-beaten benches lining the promenade that borders the town's soccer field. Every evening, she watches through the weave of trees and the crisscross of cyclone fencing as an Italian pro soccer team prepares for their fall season. Taut bodies simmer in the late summer sun. Dance of footwork brings the ball downfield. The goalie careens sideways, stretching his body and arms to stop a surefire score.

She tries to remember what it felt like to be infinite.

After sunset, these same men will stroll through the cobbled streets, sidle up to lone women window shopping along the Corso Guiseppe Mazzini, sweettalk their way into a drink or possibly more. Truth be told, she longs to be one of those women. What would she do if it happened? Nothing, she was sure. That part of her mother's Catholic faith was too ingrained in her to consider infidelity. She feels like she's spent her adult life trying to make up for her sister Helen's *mistake*, the out-of-wedlock pregnancy. Perhaps if she hadn't nursed her mother through the subsequent breakdown, she might have risked more. Could she really leave James for good? As it was, her mother believed Kate's lie that they were merely having trouble getting pregnant.

Soccer practice over, the field empties. The elderly groundskeeper hugs the steering wheel of his rusting tractor, carves the field in even stripes of dark and light, dark and light. She knows when she's gone, it won't matter that she's seen him erase each painted line, the white arc of the goalkeeper's sanctum, and the boundaries of a circumscribed world until everything is light and shadow.

At a neighboring bench along the promenade where the Spoletini make their evening *passeggiate*, she spies two old men hunched over canes carved of fallen limbs gnarled as their fingers, sipping grappa from delicate crystal glasses. Two rheumy-eyed old women open a folding table and flare a red-and-white checkered tablecloth over it, then set thick ceramic bowls of cherries in front of their men. They laugh and talk loudly, spit cherry pits on the grass, raise grappa to their lips to wash down the sweet fruit.

Overhead, a single bird's insistent chirping sounds like heartbreak.

She knows that every tomorrow after she leaves, soccer players will fill this field, and ancient men will talk of the old days, talk and drink the old days while their wives nod and smile and push bowls of ripe cherries in front of them. And she'll be gone.

But she's here, watching ants make exclamation marks on the white pavement. They, too, seem surprised by the secret song of the ordinary that plays all around her.

It's time, she knows, to leave, to make her way up Spoleto's steep hills, to her pensione overlooking the Cattedrale di Santa Maria Assunta, the town's grand duomo, where the gatekeeper guards the sullen wooden doors and fading frescoes of the

Judas kiss. She closes her eyes, conjuring the mosaic within, of Christ flanked by the saints, male and female, blessing the world. Somewhere she read of a curse associated with this church. She wonders at the simple faith of blessing and curse woven into a single fabric, and the long line of the devout carrying forward the belief in God and eternal life, in saints and sinners, in Heaven and Hell. The mosaic calls to her, but she doesn't leave the park. The encroaching dark is close, familiar.

All over the world, lights go on.

All over the world, hearts break slowly.

All over the world, the world ends for some while here, on her park bench, a teenaged couple pauses. The boy sits, the girl curls up on his lap. They hold each other tight and kiss, thinking they've invented new ways of making love.

ALL THIS THE HEART ORDAINS

At the top of a steep and winding hill in the village of Manoppello in Abruzzo lies Basilica Volto Santo, the Basilica of the Holy Face. On the altar, a monstrance displays an extraordinary relic that's been guarded by Capuchin friars for almost four hundred years. A delicate veil, sandwiched between sheets of glass and surrounded by a gilded frame, contains the imprint of a man's face. True believers swear the veil is the cloth placed over Jesus' face after His Crucifixion while He lay in His tomb. How it came to be in this hill town, so small that without the sanctuary it would be all but forgotten, is a matter of debate.

The veil is so transparent that objects placed on either side can be clearly seen through the material. Scientific study has determined that the veil is made of sea-silk. Those who believe that the veil's facial impression comes from nature—that it's an *acheiropoietos*—argue that the material is too fine to be painted. Furthermore, they assert, the unusual fluctuation of colors in varying degrees of light can only be found in nature.

Sister Blandina Pascalis Schlömer, a nun with expertise in iconography, used a process called *sopraposition* to compare the face on the Shroud of Turin, believed to be Christ's burial covering, with the Holy Face. She found the two faces identical except that the Turin eyes are closed. True believers claim that the shroud reveals His face in death, while the Manoppello veil reveals His face at the moment of the Resurrection, and that both are the last traces of His real presence on Earth. To the faithful, the veil proves that Jesus conquered death, and in His

Resurrection, promised us eternal life.

You were among those faithful, Mom. You believed both the shroud and the veil were evidence of God's miracles on earth.

*   *   *

Even near the end of my long vigil by your hospital bedside, you insisted I "make your face." So there I was, fixing your hair and applying what little makeup I carried with me. Your face was so unusually pale that my ivory foundation matched your skin perfectly. Your skin was soft, I remember that. Your skin was always soft. Years of fastidiously applying moisturizer and avoiding the sun made it so. After smoothing the foundation with my fingers, I thumbed peach blush on your cheeks and the planes of your eyelids, applied a thin edge of eyeliner, and brushed two coats of black mascara on your lashes. Your eyes were prettier than mine, deep brown instead of the washed-out blue I inherited from Dad's side of the family. I blended everything with crumpled tissues I dug out of my purse.

Finally, I gave you a compact mirror so that you could apply the red lipstick you always favored. The lipstick caught in the rough edges of your lips, the dryness coming from something parched deep inside you. In truth, the cherry red which used to highlight your olive skin and dark hair contrasted oddly with the pallor that had overtaken your complexion. You licked an index finger and smoothed each eyebrow, satisfied. Then your head fell back on the pillow and, exhausted by the effort, you closed your eyes.

When I was very young, I thought you'd been born with perfect skin, blush cheeks, and dark eyelashes because you always put on your makeup first thing in the morning before you left your bedroom. Some call it vanity. I admired that you always took the time to present a beautiful figure to the world when I rarely took the time to do so.

After they settled you into your hospital room, a nurse

handed me a plastic bag with your personal effects. My inclination was to throw the bag in the nearest trash can. Barring a miracle, what use were these things? Underneath the clothes you'd worn to the hospital was a manila envelope. Inside, sealed in a plastic bag, were the rings you always wore—the amber topaz on your right ring finger and your engagement ring with its row of tiny diamonds paired with the plain platinum wedding band on your left. I couldn't imagine you never wearing them again. They looked so different, not catching the light the way they used to when you punctuated your conversations with energetic hand gestures. Red bands tattooed your fingers where the rings used to be.

Dad had given you the topaz—your birthstone—when you were dating. When he handed you the blue velvet box, you thought it was an engagement ring. It took him another year to work up the courage to propose. Still, you slid the ring on your finger and told Dad how much you loved topaz. He'd spent a month's salary on that ring, another two months' on the wedding rings. You wore the rings to the hospital and didn't take them off until the nurse ordered you to do so.

In the bottom of the plastic bag was the rosary you carried with you, the very one we'd bought in Manoppello. A tiny impression of the Holy Face no bigger than my thumbnail graced the sterling silver medal that joined the initial string of beads to the circle of beads containing the five decades. I held the rosary up to the hospital fluorescents. Even under those harsh lights, the faceted crystal beads cast rainbows that danced across the whitewashed walls and ceiling.

*   *   *

James and I took you to Italy what was to be your last time in the summer of 2008. Was that only a decade ago? Dad didn't come. Both his knees needed replacement, and he balked at the prospect of such major surgery. He never trusted doctors. He seemed to prefer to walk hunched over, in constant pain.

We started as we always did in Roccamaro, the village from which your parents emigrated almost a century before. Our distant relatives treated us to a midday meal that lasted for hours and rivaled your Sunday afternoon extravaganzas— an antipasto of homemade cream mozzarella with crostini and Cerignola olives, fettuccine *al sugo di pomodoro*, lemon *sorbetto* to cleanse the palette, roast pork and rosemary-crusted potatoes, mixed greens (always eaten *after* the *secondo piatto*), fresh peaches and blood oranges, and finally espresso served with fried *caggionetti* oozing with chocolate-almond filling. Even at midday, wine from the village co-op flowed freely.

Francesca, an old family friend who lived in your ancestral home at the top of the hill, regaled us with stories of Roccamaro when she was a young girl. I didn't understand much, as she spoke only Italian, but I did understand the tears in your eyes— tears of laughter, tears of sorrow, tears of remembrance of your mother, whom I never knew, and the grandparents and uncle, Nonna and Papà and Antonio, whom you never met.

Toward the end of that trip, you insisted on visiting Manoppello. It was the first time I'd heard of the village, and the first time you'd asked. Your mother, you said, had told you of her annual pilgrimages to the Holy Face on the Feast of the Transfiguration, August 6th, when thousands swarmed up Via Cappuccini, attended evening Mass, and then followed the priests carrying the relic in its glass-enclosed case through the streets.

We were two weeks early for the festival, and Via Cappuccini was deserted. We parked at the bottom in front of the first of the fourteen Stations of the Cross that lined the road. A simple concrete marker enclosed a niche depicting Jesus being judged by Pontius Pilate, the governor of Judaea hesitant but ultimately giving in to the rabble who wanted Jesus condemned to death for insurrection.

You knelt down on the hard curb, and James and I flanked you kneeling as you pulled out a rosary. "In the name of the Father, and of the Son, and of the Holy Spirit," you said, making the sign of the cross with the crucifix. You nudged me, and I blessed myself, mumbled "Amen." Then we prayed together the Apostles' Creed, an Our Father, three Hail Marys, and the Glory Be.

Moving on to the first decade, you said, "The first Sorrowful Mystery is Jesus' agony in the garden."

"But don't the Joyful Mysteries come first?" I asked.

"We'll save those for the church." Which made no sense, but kneeling there, my knees an agony, I just wanted to get through the first decade.

We continued uphill, parking by the side of the road at each of the first five stations, kneeling and praying through the Sorrowful Mysteries, culminating with the Crucifixion and the final meditation, which you knew by heart: "Let us pray. O God, whose Only Begotten Son, by His life, death, and resurrection, has purchased for us the rewards of eternal life, grant, we beseech Thee, that while meditating on these mysteries of the most holy Rosary of the Blessed Virgin Mary, we may imitate what they contain and obtain what they promise, through the same Christ our Lord."

"Amen," we said in unison, then rose and returned to the car.

As we approached the Sixth Station—Veronica wipes the face of Jesus—you tapped James on the shoulder and pointed to the shrine.

"We've done the Rosary," I said.

"My mother stopped at every station and prayed through all of the mysteries. And she walked the whole way!"

"I'm already tired." I looked over at James for support.

Instead, he killed the car engine and shrugged. "We've come all this way."

Again you pulled out your rosary, and again we knelt on the curb. There was no point in arguing.

"The first Glorious Mystery," you began, "the Resurrection."

James and you prayed while I contemplated the shrine. I

knew from my days in parochial school that Veronica, showing admirable fearlessness, pushed her way through the violent crowd and the soldiers guarding the route to Calvary to wipe blood and sweat from Jesus' face. In gratitude, He bestowed the impression of His face upon the cloth.

Silence settled as we knelt there, and I realized you'd said the Glory Be to finish off the decade. "You know, Mom, Veronica is the patron saint of laundry workers," I said as we rose and stretched. "Though why a woman who kept a cloth with a permanent stain would be revered by those who labored to get stains out is the true mystery."

"Really, Kate! Such sacrilege!" But you *did* laugh. I remember that.

And so it went as we drove from one station to the next. The only respite from the heat and sun was in the grove that enclosed Stations X and XI, Jesus stripped of his clothing and Jesus nailed to the cross. We prayed through the Glorious Mysteries and the Luminous Mysteries until we arrived at the broad plaza that marked the top of the hill. There we stood before the basilica's façade and said the fifteenth and final decade.

"So no Joyful Mysteries?" I asked, thankful there were only fourteen stations, only enough for three Rosaries.

"I haven't forgotten," you said, and tucked the rosary in your purse. "I'm saving them for the Holy Face."

It did seem a miracle that, while James and I were perspiring, and all I could think of was something to eat and drink, you looked untouched—at seventy-seven, no less—by the long morning coming up the hill. As luck would have it, the basilica was closed for *riposo.* Casa del Pellegrino with its shaded outdoor tables beckoned. We ordered panini and caffè macchiatos. The dollop of frothed cream floating atop the espresso reminded me of the single cloud floating that day in an otherwise cloudless sky.

In the stillness, we were quiet, as if the café itself demanded the same reverence as the church. The whole complex was designed for the horde of pilgrims who were absent but for us.

How different it would be on August 6th, the basilica filled, Via Cappuccini thronged with the faithful, the arches of light lining the road all twinkling in the dusk. We were there out of time.

*   *   *

"Frank, Frank," you whispered.

"Dad will be here soon." I touched your cheek and held your hand.

You closed your eyes as if the effort of keeping them open was overwhelming. With your eyes closed, you looked so much more like me.

A tank by your bedside hissed life-giving oxygen through a mask covering your nose and mouth. You said you were cold, and I had the nurse retrieve warmed blankets, which we arranged over your body. Within minutes, you were perspiring, tiny beads of moisture dotting your face and threatening the makeup we'd so carefully applied. I dug farther down in my purse and found a white handkerchief, which I pressed gently against your forehead and cheeks and chin. Some of the makeup came off on the cloth, a vague impression of your face. I folded it carefully and put it back in my purse.

How fragile you looked, your hair set against your pale face and fanned out on the white pillow like a dark halo. Your hair was dyed a deep shade of brown, almost black, to cover the gray you never let the world see. A bizarre image came to me—your hair caught in Dad's ten o'clock whiskers each night before you fell asleep. He kisses your hair, inhales it, reaches for you in the darkness. You turn to him and smile. Do you close your eyes and see him only in the shadow of your eyelids? Do you breathe in his ear and moan softly and wrap your arms around him when he's finished?

Dad came in the early evening. For hours, he held your hand in both of his. A surgical mask covered his nose and mouth, but in his eyes I sensed the ephemeral—that deep and abiding love that transcended a marriage's petty difficulties and inevitable sorrows. Why had I never noticed that before?

Neither of you spoke. I suppose I'll always think of your death as a quiet thing that hovers.

*　　*　　*

In my hands is a picture of you and Dad on your wedding day, your cheeks pressed together, your faces framed by the back window of your getaway car. You look as though you've just finished laughing. Tin cans attached with strings drift behind the black car, and a shaving-cream script spells "Just Married" across the chrome bumper. The car would take you to the Bellevue Stratford Hotel where you'd spend your first night together.

In the photo, rice speckles your dark hair. Your perfect white teeth are lined up like Chiclets set between full lips, a model's smile. Dad's lips frame his crooked teeth, stained by tobacco from a cigarette habit started in his early teens. His parents never spent a dollar they didn't have to—especially on dentists or other doctors, who were, they thought, only out to find things wrong. Written on his face is an expression of vulnerability and, I imagine, trust. He'd let himself in for the unexpected, getting married. As we all do.

Your getaway photo reminds me that you were unreasonably happy once. The bliss of ignorance of all that was to come. When I look at this photograph, I think of my own marriage and the wedding album in which photo after photo, James and I are beaming. How little we knew then! Yes, it's better not to know.

I never told you that there were times we'd seriously considered divorce. The strain of our arguments over having children had taken a toll on our marriage. The lies I'd told you over the years—that we were trying even when we weren't—spared me from your nagging. And—I felt the truth would break your heart.

When James finally agreed to children, it was too late. We *did* try. Maybe it was never meant to be.

*   *   *

The basilica re-opened at two o'clock. Our first stop was the gift shop. The church sexton, who doubled as the clerk, offered you a beautiful crystal rosary, the very one you brought to the hospital. You took the beads and held them up to the shop window. It was remarkable, each bead faceted to prism light in a dozen multi-colored rays.

"It's blessed by Pope John Paul II," the sexton said in perfect English, as if you needed more convincing. You waved off having it wrapped and fingered the beads as the sexton beckoned us inside the church, illuminating lights that followed us as we made our way down the aisle toward the monstrance. From a distance we could see only shadows on the framed cloth, but as we moved closer, the outlines of a face appeared.

We stopped in front of the altar and looked up at the reliquary.

The sexton whispered, "Would you like to know the story?"

Before we could answer, he continued like the trained docent he was. "The origin of the Holy Face traces back to Jesus' tomb and the cloth placed on His face, under His shroud. Both are clearly indicated in the Gospels as the burial cloths."

You interrupted him and recited the Gospel from memory. "Then Simon Peter came along behind him and went straight into the tomb. He saw the linen that had been used to wrap Christ's body cast aside, as well as the cloth that had been placed over Jesus' face, the cloth separate from the linen."

"Yes, yes!" said the sexton.

"But how do we know this is that cloth?" I asked.

The sexton frowned. "This is the *vera icon*, the true veil."

As if that settled the matter, I thought, but held my tongue.

His account continued. "Legend has it that the veil made a

long journey from Jerusalem to Camulia in Cappadocia, where it was venerated for centuries until unbelievers threatened it. From there it traveled to Constantinople and then on to Rome, where it was stored for hundreds of years in Old St. Peter's. In 1508 it was taken to Manoppello for safekeeping during the basilica's reconstruction. If you look closely, you'll notice a shard of glass embedded in the cloth that's said to have been part of the Roman monstrance.

"In any case, an anonymous pilgrim came to the church where Dr. Giacomo Leonelli and his friends were sitting outside deep in conversation. The pilgrim pulled the good doctor inside the church, handed him a bundle, and told him that the relic within was very dear to him and that God would grant him many favors if he cared for it. The pilgrim withdrew to the holy water font while Doctor Leonelli opened the parcel. Inside he beheld a sheer cloth with the sacred image of the face of Christ impressed upon it. At first, he was frightened, but he composed himself and rewrapped the cloth. He turned to thank the pilgrim, but the man had disappeared. He went outside and asked his friends if they'd seen the pilgrim leave, but no. Everyone judged the mysterious pilgrim to be an angel. Some say it was Saint Michael himself."

"How do we know any of this is true?" I asked.

You looked at me, a trace of anger on your face.

"A doubting Thomas, eh?" The sexton laughed.

"I mean, it's just that—"

"Enough," you said.

"No, no, it's all right. Many who see still do not believe. There are other stories surrounding the provenance of the veil, but the one I'm telling you is the official history documented in 1640."

"Go on," you said, pressing your finger to my lips to silence me.

And so he did. "Leonelli preserved the cloth in his home, paying it the utmost respect as did his descendants. That is, until 1608, when a soldier married to a Leonelli woman stole the cloth and treated it badly. The cloth fell into ruin, and bad luck dogged the family until the soldier ended up on the wrong side of the law and was imprisoned. His wife was forced to sell the veil to Doctor Antonio De Fabritiis to bail out her husband. The doctor gave it to the Capuchins in 1638, and we hold it to this day."

He pointed to a set of marble stairs. "Go up there and look closely." Turning to me, he said, "Then see what you believe."

We mounted the short flight that led behind the altar to a prie-dieu. There was barely room for two, so James stood behind us while you and I knelt. I have to admit that the image was striking in its clarity. The eyes were brown and melancholy, the nose canted as if it had been broken and healed that way, the lips parted as if in the act of speaking. The face was composed, peaceful. No trace remained of the ordeal that the man who owned the face had just endured, other than a slight swelling on the right cheek and a few brown splotches that could be construed as dried blood.

"Next thing you know, the eyes will be following us," I said.

"Shush," you whispered.

I looked back at James, who mouthed "indulge her."

With your new rosary in hand, we prayed the Joyful Mysteries. I folded my hands and murmured along as I examined the veil. I thought that if I simply stared long enough, the truth of its provenance would become clear. I wanted your deep faith.

What was strange about the cloth was that the colors in the image *did* change as I moved my head back and forth. Was it a trick of the light? Later I learned that a painted object doesn't have this quality, further "proof" that this image was from nature. That there was enough radiation at the moment of resurrection to make this mystical impression. And then I saw that there was, indeed, a sliver of glass in the corner of the cloth.

After we finished the final Glory Be, you took three holy cards from a wooden box next to the monstrance and handed one each to James and me. In tiny print at the bottom was a promise of five hundred indulgences in exchange for saying the prayer. Ironically, it was the Prayer for Immigrants. "*O Gesù,*" you read in perfect Italian, "*che dai primi giorni della Tua vita terrena hai lasciato il Tuo luogo natio con Maria...*" Pausing, you started again, translating the prayer for us into English. "O Jesus, who from the first days of Your earthly life left Your native place with Mary, Your tender Mother, and with Joseph endured in Egypt the pains and hardships of poor emigrants, turn Your gaze to our brothers and sisters who, far from their beloved homeland and from all that is dearest to them, are forced to struggle in the midst of serious difficulties and are often exposed to numerous dangers and pitfalls for their souls. Lord, be a guide to them on the uncertain path. Help in fatigue, comfort in sorrows. Preserve them in the integrity of faith, in holiness of morals, and in affection for children, spouses, and parents, that one day not far away they may be reunited with their loved ones in this earthly homeland and then live reunited forever in the heavenly homeland. Amen."

"Amen," James and I chorused. What was the harm in indulging you after all?

Before you rose from the kneeler, you pressed your hand against the glass, covering the wound on Jesus' cheek. Tearing up as you stared into the Holy Face, you nodded your head, then blessed yourself.

*   *   *

As you were taken away in the ambulance that last time, gasping for air, I felt as if I were suffocating too. If only my breath could have saved you. But no. It's not for a daughter to save her mother, nor to live her mother's other possible lives.

In the hospital, my nose and mouth covered by a surgical mask for your protection, I watched you struggle for breath and felt like I could hardly breathe. Beads of moisture collected on the inside surface of your oxygen mask and streaked down the plastic, some quickly, some slowly. They traced patterns inside the mask that reminded me of lace.

You pulled the mask from your face and placed your hand on my forearm. "I'd like to see Italy one last time," you said. "Just once more."

Of course, it was impossible. Your request reminded me of the time you'd held the hand of one of your cousins as he lay in this very same hospital dying of brain cancer and spoke of returning to the old country. You reassured him by saying "certainly you will!"

Was that less cruel than me holding your hand and saying nothing?

*　　*　　*

I was eight when Kennedy was assassinated. It happened while I sat beneath your ironing board, making a tent of the long white tablecloth you were starching for Thanksgiving. Pop-Pop was napping in his wheelchair by the window. The TV was tuned to the afternoon soaps—*As the World Turns* or *Search for Tomorrow* or *The Guiding Light*, I don't remember exactly. Those shows all blended together into one continuous sob story. But I do remember you pausing in your work, the steady rhythm of the iron above my head interrupted by the news bulletin. Kennedy, the first Catholic president, had been shot in Dallas.

We all know the story now, or think we know. Lee Harvey Oswald, a lone shooter trained in the art of war, takes out the president from a lonely observation post atop a book depository above a grassy knoll. Or the Russians hired Oswald. Or he was a CIA stooge. Theories abound. No one knows the full truth of that November day.

You took the news badly, forgetting the hot iron. It left a perfect triangular scorch mark on the white cloth.

You believed in Camelot. You thought JFK was one of your own simply because he was Catholic. That the world, giving up its prejudices, was changing for the better. Never mind that the Kennedy family allegedly earned part of their fortune through bootlegging during Prohibition. Never mind that Dad made in a year what JFK might spend on a rare bottle of wine. Never mind Marilyn Monroe, for that matter.

Images come unbidden, inextricably linked: Jackie cradling her husband in the limo and trying to push his brains back into his head, her pink suit stained with blood. Next the pietà, Mary holding the dead Jesus, blood dripping from His five wounds. Then you, holding me, trying to stop my blood with your treasured scarf.

I hardly remember the instant I plunged through our plate-glass storm door. I was running from you. I'd done something wrong, but I can't remember what it was, only that the deed must have been so terrible and I so frightened of your wrath that I ran right through the glass. There was blood everywhere and Dad called the ambulance and you pulled a jagged piece of glass from my forearm and tourniquetted the scarf you were wearing around my upper arm, your favorite scarf, you thought it made you look like Jackie O, a fake Hermès you'd gotten on the streets of New York City, gold and white with blue anchors on it, made of polyester though the vendor assured you it was silk, and it became soaked with my blood, I was nauseous with the sight of blood flowing down my arm and onto the shattered glass and concrete stoop, and I couldn't believe how I could bleed so, so very red and Dad shouting into the phone for the ambulance to *hurry up* and repeating our name and address and you held me and prayed one Hail Mary after another until the ambulance came and they put me on a stretcher and the EMTs took over and I lifted my head to wave weakly through the ambulance's back doors and you waved back with the bloody scarf the EMTs had replaced with a band of rubber and you and Dad were framed in those doors and Dad had his arm around your shoulders and you had your arm around his waist and one hand to your mouth and just as the doors were closing, you put your head on his shoulder and he put his hand on your head and twined his fingers through your thick, black hair and you were probably crying and he kissed your hair as the siren wailed and the doors shut tight and the ambulance sped away.

Sometimes I wonder if lives echo themselves down through the generations. How many times had you told me the story of that Ash Wednesday when you were ten, how you refused to accompany your mother to church for the smudged cross of ashes and punctuated your refusal by smashing the wooden crucifix that hung over your parents' bed? You ran from her back hand, down the stairs and out the front door and off the curb into the street. For your transgressions, God immediately punished you—a Bond Bread truck out making deliveries knocked you down and ran over your forehead. I can see your mother holding your limp body in the street as you bled onto her fine church clothes, praying Hail Marys as she waited for an ambulance to take you to the hospital.

You often told me that I reminded you of your mother. The way I laughed, the way I stood with my hands on my hips, the set of my jaw.

Her white nightgown, the one she made and wore on her wedding night, the one you wore on yours, the one I refused to wear on mine, rests on a headless dummy in the corner of my spare bedroom, and there she is, the woman I knew only through stories, waiting for me to speak.

*　　*　　*

There's a photograph you kept on the mantel, the only one of your mother and father and their firstborn son, Luca. In it, he's almost four. A piece of chocolate, a bribe from your mother to hold still for the photograph, melts in his hand. Your father is smiling, but your mother and Luca are tight-lipped. Their expressions belie a certain sadness, as if they had known what was to be. It's the only picture of my lost uncle. Not long after this photo was taken, he died in Italy of typhoid fever. Your mother spent every day of her life afterward mourning her son. And yet she didn't curse God for her greatest misfortune.

At the time the picture was taken, your father had been in America for almost five years, hoarding the money he earned as a tailor to bring his wife and son to the United States in first class. Hoarding is perhaps not the right word. Vincent, as he called himself in America, was also *patrono* in his West Philadelphia neighborhood, sponsoring a score of newly-arriving immigrants. Both his desire for your mother and Luca to emigrate in style and his money-lending were indicative of his pride, but he also possessed the sort of courage and faith required to abandon what was easy and familiar.

Luca was born after Vincent departed for America. My grandfather never touched his son, never held him, never kissed him. So how is this photograph possible? If one looks carefully, one sees that my grandfather is a cutout from another photo carefully pasted so that his arm is draped around your mother's shoulders. For years I thought it was a picture of your parents and your brother, my Uncle Vinnie, and I couldn't figure out why you were missing from the photo since you were the oldest. And finally, of course, I understood the truth.

* * *

At your viewing, I slipped the topaz and the wedding rings on your fingers. Then I knelt on the prie-dieu beside your coffin and prayed the Joyful Mysteries with the Holy Face rosary, hearing your voice in my head, *Hail Mary, full of grace.* I knelt there quietly for a long time, looking at your face, composed and peaceful, no mark of the suffering you'd endured before your death. Finally, I entwined the rosary in your folded hands and watched the undertakers close the coffin lid.

* * *

I returned to Italy solo in 2018, six years after your death. James stayed behind. He said he understood. There was a time I'd thought of leaving him and fled to Spoleto alone to consider what I wanted of my future. That time was gone. This time, I wished to be alone to retrace the trip the three of us had made together. I wasn't quite sure what I hoped to gain.

Distance is, for those of us fortunate enough to be the children of children of hard-working immigrants, a span bridged by comparative wealth, the speed of travel, the ease with which we can experience foreign places and return to the familiar. I think about distance when I think of your father and his firstborn son. I imagine a bridge that might somehow have connected them—a fiction he created with the photograph on the mantel, a fiction I've created repeatedly in my mind like so many other fictions.

A long road winds up the steep hill to Roccamaro, a road once dirt now paved and connected to highways that connect to the autostrada that leads to Rome. But I can imagine Roccamaro in 1915, my grandfather Vincent courting my grandmother Anna, the two walking every day downhill into a forest of ilex. And I can imagine later, after your father left for America, your mother and her father sitting in the shade of the bougainvillea canopying the alcove that framed their front door, she weaving delicate lace and he plunging needles into fine fabric to craft the best men's suits.

When I arrived at our ancestral home at the top of Roccamaro's hill, an ancient woman opened the door, the very same woman whom we'd met during that midday feast a decade ago.

"Kate," she said, and hugged me the Italian way, giving me a kiss on each cheek.

I returned the embrace and two air kisses. "Francesca," I said, pulling her name from memory.

She let go of me and took two steps back. "*Sembri così tanto tua nonna*," she said, shaking her head and placing a hand over her mouth.

"*Grazie mille*," I said, exhausting most of my rudimentary

Italian with these two words.

She showed me from room to room, speaking rapidly in Italian, gesturing at objects as if her words and possessions meant something to me. If I were honest, the home wasn't much. The ceilings were cracked, the floors and tiles stained with age, the wallpaper faded and peeling. An enormous crystal chandelier hung above the dining table, a relic of the past, each pendant layered with dust. The house smelled pungent, odors of garlic and onion and something unidentifiable underneath.

Francesca opened French doors that led out to a narrow balcony enclosed with a filigreed iron railing. From there, I took in the unchanging view of the surrounding hill towns—Ari and Villamagna, San Pietro and Sant'Agata and Manoppello. I tried to imagine the courage it took to leave the familiar comforts of this village for the new world. So much easier to stay in one place, fixed as a star, letting the world turn around you.

San Ponziano stood across from the house. I asked the church's caretaker for directions to the graveyard where my ancestors were buried. The cemetery was on the outskirts of town, down the hill and through a stone arch. I wandered among the headstones and mausoleums until I found the family burial plot set off with an iron fence. Luca's headstone, the smallest one, stood bathed in the shade of a cypress tree. Within the same confines were the graves of your maternal grandparents who lived to old age and died of natural causes, my great-aunt Ernestina, who died of the Spanish flu, and my great-uncle Antonio, whose mind was forever scarred by his service in the First World War. It was strangely comforting to see the five of them together and know that they would never be alone.

Finally, it was time to make my pilgrimage to the Basilica of the Holy Face. Since our last visit, I'd done more research, thinking knowledge would somehow rekindle my faith. Unfortunately, the preponderance of the evidence supported unbelievers. They insisted sea-silk could indeed be painted and that the Holy Face was a medieval watercolor; that the only true veil was the one with which Veronica wiped Jesus' face, and that her veil had been continuously safeguarded in Rome ever since she gifted it to Emperor Tiberius; that the Catholic Church never declared the Holy Face a true relic because it hadn't produced any proven miracles; and so forth.

It was early morning, the sun just coming up when I parked my rental car at the base of Via Cappuccini. I forgot to bring a rosary—truth be told, unlike you, I never carried one—but as you used to say, that's why God gave us ten fingers. I decided to walk the whole way, as my maternal forebears did, stopping at each Station of the Cross and praying through all the mysteries, saving the joyful ones for the Holy Face as we did years ago.

As I prayed, I smiled to myself, thinking of the many indulgences these prayers could be earning for you and all those who had gone before. Hundreds and hundreds of indulgences! Did my Rosaries still count considering my doubts? In any case, I thought, you'd lived a virtuous life and—if God were just—you'd earned your way into heaven without my paltry prayers.

When I reached the cobbled plaza in front of the basilica, Casa del Pellegrino beckoned. But it was getting near noon, and I wanted to complete my mission before the church closed for *riposo*. The sexton was nowhere to be found, but the doors were open and the lights were on, so I walked up the central aisle toward the altar, my eyes fixed on the reliquary. As I approached, the Holy Face came into focus—the same peace in His open eyes, as if He'd just awakened. The closer I came the more details appeared—the crooked nose, the tips of His incisor teeth, the edema on His cheek. Walking up the short flight of steps to the prie-dieu behind the altar, I knelt and looked frankly at the face that stared back at me. I said the Joyful Mysteries, took a holy card, and mouthed the Prayer for Immigrants in ersatz Italian.

My knees ached, but still I knelt there, my hands folded in prayer. I thought about you. I thought about your mother and your mother's mother. I thought about the daughter—having waited too long—that I could never have. Then I blessed myself and pressed my hand against the glass to cover the bloodstain on Christ's cheek. And Mom, I swear, it was warm to the touch.

ABOUT THE AUTHOR

Cynthia Reeves is the author of three books of fiction. In addition to the novel in stories *Falling Through the New World*, her major works include the novel *The Last Whaler* (Regal House Publishing, September 2024) and the novella *Badlands* (Miami University Press, 2008). *The Last Whaler* follows a widower-whaler's journey to a remote fjord on Svalbard as he comes to terms with his past and the impact of his beluga whaling on once-pristine shores. *Badlands*, awarded Miami University Press's Novella Prize, portrays a night of crisis during which a dying woman attempts to reconcile her part in covering up a significant find at an archaeological excavation at Wounded Knee. In part, the novella gives voice to 136 "disappeared" Lakota, victims of the Wounded Knee Massacre.

Reeves's fiction, poetry, and essays have appeared widely. She has been awarded residencies to the Arctic Circle's 2017 Summer Solstice and 2024 Alumni Expeditions, Hawthornden Castle, Galleri Svalbard, Art & Science in the Field, and Vermont Studio Center. A graduate of Warren Wilson's MFA program, she taught in Bryn Mawr College's Creative Writing Program and Rosemont College's MFA program. She lives with her husband in Camden, Maine.

Cynthia Reeves's expertly crafted novel in stories finds artistry in manual labor and reveals the sacred in the everyday. Twists of lace ribbon, a tailor's steady stitching, thread looped into intricate patterns to make a wedding or mourning veil, a string of rosary beads, notches in a wooden tabletop marking time and human presence: Reeves uses these heirlooms and artifacts to seamlessly bind generations of an Italian-American family, old country to new, past to present. *Falling Through the New World* is a deeply moving story of the Desiderio family—a history in handwork that is the truest expression of faith in the future.

—Elizabeth Mosier, author of *Excavating Memory: Archaeology and Home*

Spanning four generations and two continents, the richly textured stories of *Falling Through the New World* explore the costs and promise of emigration from rural Italy to urban America. With meticulous and moving detail, Reeves depicts characters struggling to reconcile the beauty of their parents' customs and faith with their increasing irrelevance in the modern world. Members of the Italian-American diaspora and anyone who has sought a similar reconciliation with the past will find in this collection a voice of wisdom and compassion.

—Laura Bonazzoli, author of *Consecration Pond: A Novel in Stories*

In richly described scenes, Cynthia Reeves traces familial patterns across time and continents. War, migration, illness, faith and faithlessness drive four generations of an Italian family apart and together. Reeves's characters endure, somehow, the great tragedies of the early twentieth century and live on through the patterns they create—the dance of marriage, the intricate lace her female characters weave, and other acts of faith and dedication. In such a slim volume—resplendent with highly textured scenes of domesticity—Reeves creates a testament to the fortitude of our immigrant forebears that is at once heartbreaking and uplifting.

—Margaret Luongo, author of *History of Art* and *If the Heart Is Lean*